MAN-MADE
TWO A NEW LIFE

CASSIE CLUSTER

Published by Picky Press.

Contents

Chapter	Page
Prologue	1
1 A New Beginning	5
2 Merging Lives	13
3 Dr. Betty's Diagnosis	21
4 Betty's Future Plans	29
5 The Procedure	39
6 Melissa's Plot	47
7 Fourth of July Picnic	55
8 Announcing the News	65
9 Just a Walk in the Park	71
10 Robot for Ransom	81
11 Betty's Legacy	91
12 Recovery	99
13 Fate	107
14 Eyewitness	115
15 A Time to Move On	125

16 Going Green — 135

17 It's Hard to Say Goodbye — 145

18 Question and Answer Time — 155

19 The Farewell Party Ends — 163

20 Preparing to Move — 173

21 A New Battle — 181

22 What to Do? — 189

23 Hiding Out in the Restroom — 199

24 This Too Is for the Best — 205

Prologue

In the very near future, man-made certified caregiving nurses with artificial intelligence (AI) are the norm. Insusceptible to pandemics and able to work tirelessly around the clock, they are the answer to any medical crisis.

The Caring Corporation had developed into a huge medical plaza, featuring cutting-edge technology and on-site patient care. It was originally started by a father and son team: Dr. Kenneth Kerring, a logical, yet sensitive prosthetist, and his shy, intellectual son Dr. Robert Kerring, who dealt with robotics and AI. They perfected the caregiver models, which aside from computer brains, also had living, semi-organic cell-cultured skin.

In this, the second of the Man-Made trilogy, our story again centers around Betty, the original G-4 prototype.

Betty had always been the Kerrings' sentimental favorite. However, Robert had experimented with Betty's original programming, to allow Betty to tweak her own educational coding even further, enabling her to make independent medical decisions. Instead of merely enhancing her learning capabilities, it also resulted in her having the coding equivalent to human emotions. Betty questioned this development at first, thinking there was something very wrong with her, but eventually she came to deal with this unusual "side effect."

Betty still had the ability to communicate with other machines and computer systems, send files to her cloud-based storage accounts, and could contact people by text or phone, all using her computer mind.

Betty was bought for use as a flight attendant by James Simmons, the Chief Human Resources Officer, and CPA for Quality First Airlines. Jimmy abused her badly. Unfortunately, Betty's programming didn't allow her to defend herself. She could only intervene to defend and protect others but could not harm any other beings outright.

Betty became a recognized heroine for saving many people's lives. She intervened and prevented a hijacking attempt, which won her a Single Act of Heroism Citizen Honors Award for her bravery. She eventually sued Jimmy, was granted her freedom and the legal status of "personhood" by the New York State Supreme Court. Betty's genuineness of emotions had been confirmed by two forensic psychologists called upon as expert witnesses, as well as many other character witnesses, including fellow flight crew members. Even Jasper Coates, the owner of Quality First, testified on Betty's behalf, against his own nephew Jimmy!

All G-4 models that Caring Corp. created had individual 3-D printed faces based on decedents from the Social Security Death Index. Each one was unique. Betty's face happened to be based on the late wife of her faithful civil rights attorney, Mack Schwartz.

Needless to say, between Betty's charming personality, and Mack's late wife's face, he just couldn't help but fall in love with her. When Betty was a flight attendant, she fell for Mack the moment she first saw him. To help with Betty's case, they got married in a civil ceremony, since there was no US law stating that a human and a robot could not marry.

The happy couple had to adhere to some extra strictures, since Mack was an Orthodox Jew. For religious and other reasons, their relationship was purely platonic. It just proved that theirs was one of the purest forms of love imaginable.

Aside from Mack, the closest thing Betty had to a family, were her creators the Kerrings. Dr. Kenneth was much like a father, and "Robbie" was just like a brother to her.

Betty had two close friends: Tom Grady, a co-pilot for Quality First, who's aunt Leela was in the Caring Corp. Hospice Center. She took care of her, and they became close until she died, leaving Betty heartbroken and no longer wanting to work there. Being a romantic at heart, Betty intervened to get her best friend Meg and Tom together, culminating in their getting married.

Jimmy and his con-artist girlfriend Melissa, had devised a scheme to embezzle money from Quality First, making it appear to be taxes taken out of employee wages. Melissa was working for a man named Gio, a fact that Jimmy did not yet know. Betty contacted the bank and the legal authorities to intervene, so the money would be returned to Jasper and ultimately paid back to the rightful owners.

During Betty's freedom trial, Jimmy tried to assault her in the courtroom. He was arrested and taken away.

And now, the unique story of Betty and Mack continues, *Two a New Life*.

Chapter 1
A New Beginning

After Betty's personhood trial, she and Mack headed to his apartment followed by their friends. They were all escorted by several police officers, ensuring they wouldn't be intercepted by any robot-hating protestors. As they left the parking garage, Betty noticed there was something following along at the same speed in the sky. She zoomed in to see it with her telescopic vision.

"Mack? I don't want to alarm you, but there's a small drone following us. It may be weaponized," Betty said calmly.

"Really?" Mack started to get worried. "Now the robot haters are spying on us to see where we go! Who'd think they'd harass us by air. How hypocritical. They criticize technology, saying it takes away jobs, yet they have no problem using it to invade privacy and harm people! Where is it? I don't even see it."

"It's best not to draw attention by looking at it. It may provoke them to attack, then others can get hurt as well. I have a plan." Betty scanned for various radio frequencies and was able to pick up on the offending drone. It was very primitive, an older model using the same range as a phone. She contacted the officers using her computer mind, and they notified a police helicopter.

As they reached an area where there were few buildings and no people, the drone started coming in close enough that even Mack could see it. It had a video camera with some sort of firing device attached to its top, and it now appeared to be singling out Mack's autonomous robocar. Betty's processors sped up, so that time slowed down for her. She did some quick calculations on velocity and momentum, and just as the drone started to swoop toward them, she locked onto its signal and proceeded to jam it by broadcasting her loudest alert alarm possible onto the drone's exact frequency. It was enough to send it hurdling off to crash on the side of the road, away from any traffic or pedestrians.

Mack was nearly holding his breath in suspense as the drone was chasing them, and he let out a huge sigh of relief.

Betty finished up her conversation she was having with the officers then turned to Mack, now speaking to him audibly.

"They'll cross reference the drone's serial number to its owner, and the perpetrator will be arrested. Now, let's get home!"

On the way, Betty placed a delivery order from a recently opened local kosher Chinese restaurant in her mind:

"*. . . And please make sure to include eight fortune cookies and seven pairs of chopsticks. Thank you!*"

Undeterred from the close call, Betty's victory party ensued, celebrating her new status of having equal rights and the same freedom as any human being. Those in attendance were her best friend Meg Grady with her husband Tom, Meg's parents Jasper and Becky Coates, and Drs. Kenneth and Robert Kerring.

Betty delighted in watching them all attempt to eat their food, as most fumbled with maneuvering their chopsticks. Their lack of dexterity was amusing to everyone. The night was filled with laughter and good conversation. Jasper and Dr. Kerring started to reminisce about their college days together.

"Kenny, do you remember when we were both vying for the same girl; that snobby one named Domonique?" Jasper chuckled. "We both asked her out. Uh, that was before I met you Honey," he said looking at Becky sweetly. She motioned him to go on; smiled and rolled her eyes, as Meg giggled.

"We each thought she had agreed to be our girlfriend, but she dumped us both when that handsome football player came along. And you were crying? That's when he first called you the nickname, 'Crybaby Kerring.' " Jasper jokingly frowned.

Robert exclaimed, "Dad, you never told me about that!"

"You didn't need to threaten him on my account!" Dr. Kerring put his hand next to his mouth and whispered, "Although I did secretly appreciate that." Then he sighed and continued louder, "I know, I take things too seriously. But I met Cara the very next day and the rest was history. You're a good man Jasp."

At the end of the meal, every person got a fortune cookie. They took turns going around the table, each breaking open their cookie and reading their fortune aloud. It was great fun.

"'You will live long and prosper,' " Mack related his fortune to them. "Well, that's always a good thing." He smiled.

"It sounds like that one was written by a 'Star Trek' fan," Tom mused. He then read his aloud, "'You will always be surrounded by true friends.' I like that. And may we have many more parties like this one to make that come true. Here's to a new life for Betty and Mack!" Those with drinks clinked their glasses together affirming the toast.

"'Experience is the best teacher,'" Jasper stated his. "Yup, I can certainly relate to that one." He looked at Becky sadly thinking about his dealings with his swindling nephew Jimmy.

Becky nodded in agreement with hers. "'You love peace.'"

Betty held her cookie up. "Can someone please eat my cookie for me?" Everyone laughed as she proceeded to read hers.

"'In dreams and in love, there are no impossibilities.' Wow, these are very accurate!" She smiled radiantly, looking at Mack.

"'He who throws dirt is losing ground,'" Dr. Kenneth Kerring announced his. Everyone agreed it was a good saying.

"You would get a logical one Dad," Robert quipped.

Dr. Kerring thought a moment, stroking his stubbly beard.

"Hmm. To throw the dirt, as with a rake-like tool, it would ultimately help to aerate the soil. That may just enhance the growth of my Peppergrape plants. That would be a good thing!"

"Kenny, you're always just too literal. Dirt is a synonym for ground. But 'losing ground,' is basically diminishing one's position. So, if you 'throw dirt,' you lose your ranking or good status." Jasper laughed heartily. "This man's a genius and I still have to explain it to him!"

Betty asked, "Isn't 'throwing dirt' figuratively speaking

badly about someone?" She cocked her head looking at Mack.

"Yes Betty. And it is something that should never be done," Mack acknowledged. "Who's reading the next one?"

"I'll go," Robert chimed in. "'Expect the unexpected.'" He snickered. "Now I know that directly corresponds to my relationship with Betty." He pointed and winked at her.

"My turn!" Meg had intentionally waited until last and broke open her cookie. "'Happy news is on its way.' Oh, my goodness!" She was almost in tears but had a huge smile.

"Actually, I do have good news to share, Tom already knows. I was waiting for the perfect time. Momma, Daddy?" She went over to Becky and Jasper. "You're going to be grandparents!" In typical Meg fashion, she started jumping up and down for joy.

"I'm going to be an aunt?" Betty shrieked, jumping with her.

"You'll be an awesome aunt!" Meg hugged her.

The victory party eventually ended, and all left happy and satisfied with renewed hopes for the future.

A few weeks after the trial, things would settle down a bit, then Betty and Mack would finally be safer from threats or violence of the robot-hating protestors. Betty would no longer be news and people would forget. Fortunately, the public eye tended to have a very short attention span. It was also good that Mack had a very private, secure apartment. Now they could finally relax a bit and live their lives anew as a happily married couple, even if it was only "on paper."

Living with someone new is always a big adjustment. Both Betty and Mack had their own unique habits. Mack still slept on the couch. He was set in his ways and had to go do his "Jewish stuff" every morning. No longer a slave, Betty loved this new concept of "a man must honor his wife more than himself." Still, she wanted to take care of Mack. It was her nature as a caregiver.

As time went on, Betty finally confronted Mack about something that had bothered her for a very long time.

"Why do you tell strangers who know I was man-made, that I look just like your late wife? It kind of hurts me, Mack. Why do you have to say that to people?" Betty looked at him sadly. "You know I would have loved Miri, but she is gone."

"I know Betty," Mack knew she deserved an explanation.

"It's for this reason only," he said, pointing in the air. "Most people don't understand our relationship; they view a robot as being a non-living being or a glorified appliance. Of course, I don't see you that way. They don't know you like I do. But, by telling them that you look like her, it's perhaps the only thing humans can relate to." Mack looked her in the eyes.

"When I first found out you were man-made, to be quite honest, I almost wondered about my own sanity when I started having feelings for you." He looked down. "But you demonstrated your emotions, your bravery, and caring for others. How could I not help but fall in love with you . . . for you Betty?"

She felt much better after that, and finally understood.

Mack turned toward her and looked into her eyes, since he knew she could read him for sincerity and honesty.

"I'll tell you a secret I didn't want to admit, even to myself. I believe you are even braver than Miri was. She was more passive. But you know when to be passive and when to take direct action. I know you don't like confrontation, but you will confront people if necessary. You stood up to the hijackers and faced Jimmy in court. That takes courage!"

"I knew you were special too Mack, when I first saw you sitting in your seat 5A on the plane. I even remarked to Gita Brothers that you were cute." She giggled. "I had a strange urge to take care of you over all the other passengers. I think it may be a phenomenon they call 'love at first sight,'" Betty said shyly.

"I know you worry that I see you as Miri's substitute." Mack smiled at her with loving eyes. "There's nothing to worry about! Your unique personality eclipses hers. And to be honest, your voice is much more pleasant." Betty's processors tickled with joy.

"Little did I know then how much you would help me in the future! I can't thank you enough for the priceless gift of freedom that you gave me. I wish there was something as special I could give you in return," she said with a thoughtful twinkle in her eyes.

Mack replied, "Just stay the way you are. Everything should fall into place. I think the two of us will have such a happy future together. If you really want to be a paralegal, that would be so wonderful! We can work together to make sure those who need representation, can have the same rights as anyone else."

During the time Betty had to wait in Mack's apartment before the trial, she read Mack's extensive library of books, from the "Talmud" and Jewish law to psychology and civil law. Her AI was in full learning mode, absorbing all the information like a sponge, and scanning everything into her memory banks for future reference. A week after the trial she became a certified paralegal, just as Mack's late wife Miri would have done, had she survived the accident that took her short life.

Betty then did legal research for Mack whenever he needed. He still took regular flights to Des Moines, although much less often. His mother lived there, and he also had a small private practice. Mack visited his mother when he could. Unfortunately, she seemed to be suffering from dementia and didn't always recognize him. On bad days she needed help to remember.

Mack's brother Barry was twenty years older than he was and tried to help by getting their mother into a nursing home where she could be cared for. After their father was killed in a freak accident at a kosher meat packing plant six years earlier, Barry stopped being religious, withdrew and rarely spoke to Mack.

Shortly before Mack lost Miri, he lost his father. Over the last few years, his mother was mentally slipping away, and Barry didn't keep in touch. Was it any wonder why, when Betty first met him, she referred to Mack as "the Sad Man"?

Fortunately, once he really "saw" Betty, that all changed.

Chapter 2
Merging Lives

It had been about three weeks since Betty's official personhood trial to gain her freedom, so they thought it was finally safe for them both to venture out together. This week, Mack decided to have Betty travel along with him to Des Moines, so she could get somewhat familiar with the new case he was working on. While they were there, Mack and Betty went to visit his mother in the nursing home.

They arrived in a rental car, parked in the lot, then went to the reception desk. Mack signed in, showing his ID. The staff was newer, and one of the workers there was a Caring Corp. model. Betty recognized her from a few years earlier.

"Kathy? What are you doing here?" Betty ran over to hug her. "I haven't seen you around in ages!"

"I was hired to come here. Caring Corp. does send models out to other locations at times. I'm sure Mr. Schwartz had something to do with it." Kathy smiled sweetly at him.

"He taught me a bit about kosher food and his Sabbath day, and what could and couldn't be done. Mostly I think he wanted someone loyal and trustworthy to take extra good care of his mother, Liora. She's a real sweetheart. Like mother, like son," Kathy chirped with the same familiar enthusiasm that Caring Corp. models typically exhibited.

"Well, I may have had a little something to do with it." Mack smiled bashfully. "My experiences with the Caring Corp. models years ago were so good that I put in a request with the nursing home. Since they were short staffed at the time, they went along with it. I think they were assigned a few others too."

Betty felt the strangest little prick of jealousy, that Mack could ever request the help of a model other than herself.

Why do I feel this? Kathy would not view Mack in the same way as I do, she thought. *Besides, he did not even know me back when Kathy first came here. I think this is an illogical emotion and I should choose to ignore it*. She got a bit upset at herself.

"Are you okay Betty?" Mack asked. She was staring into space analyzing her conflicting emotional thoughts.

"I think maybe I am just a bit nervous meeting your mother for the first time." She turned to Kathy and said, "After all, we are mare . . . " Mack quickly rushed down the hallway in an effort to get her away from Kathy.

"Gotta go. See you later Kathy!" Betty waved to her.

As they went down the hallway, she whispered to Mack, "Why did you do that? I wasn't finished talking to Kathy."

"Do we really have to explain it all? I mean, how can your friend Kathy really understand? She doesn't have the same emotions that you do." Mack thought it was a logical reason.

"Mack, are you embarrassed to be married to me? Let me

see your eyes!" Betty insisted and had him turn to face her.

"Of course not! Betty, do you not believe me when I tell you that I love you for you? Don't you trust me? You really need to prove it to yourself?" Mack looked a bit hurt.

She was satisfied that Mack was sincere by observing his reactions. There being no presence of any contradictory micro-expressions, she could see he was being truthful. Again, she was wondering why she was feeling a bit threatened by the presence of Kathy being there because of Mack's intervention.

"You don't have feelings for her do you Mack?" She looked at him cocking her head.

Mack frowned, saying, "Not like I have for you. She's just a friendly caregiver model who helps Ma out. Nothing more. Why would you even think that, Betty? You sound, jealous! That's not a good trait to have. I only love you. Please don't give it another thought. She's a friend, nothing more. You, I love with all my heart. Now let's go meet Ma."

Mack sighed, looking at her with sincere concern. "I don't mean this in a bad way. But If I didn't know any better, I'd think you were a bit hormonal! And I know that's impossible."

Mack and Betty finally arrived at Mrs. Schwartz's apartment.

"This is it. Are you ready Betty?" She nodded yes, and Mack knocked on the door. A shorter, older woman in a scarf answered.

"Hi Ma, it's me, Mack. I brought someone to meet you!" He hugged his mother and went in.

"Miri! You finally brought Miri to visit me! How are you Honey, it's been such a long time!" she remarked as she placed her hands on Betty's cheeks and kissed her forehead.

"Maccabee, you should have brought Miri to visit much sooner." His mother motioned for them to come and sit with her to talk. She was smiling and happy.

Betty looked at Mack with a slightly puzzled expression, but she knew exactly what was going on. She had seen it before in the elderly patients who had either Alzheimer's or dementia. Sometimes, there were good days, where the patient could recognize their relatives, or bad days when they couldn't remember anything. It was always so sad when they didn't.

However, in this case, was it good or bad? Betty decided to play along and pretend that she was Miri. She thought, *Why not bring a sweet old lady some joy. Let her believe I'm someone she cares about. It is most beneficial to the patient.*

Apparently today, the presence of "Miri" together with Mack, was enough to jog Mrs. Schwartz's memory. She just remained unaware of the year, or the recollection of sad events that had transpired for Miri. From her perspective, it had just been a very long time since Miri had come to visit.

"I have some cookies there in the kitchen. Can I offer you both a cup of tea, or some milk?" She got up and went to the small kitchenette, not giving them a chance to refuse.

"I'm sorry Betty. I was going to introduce you as my

wife, but it seems she already thinks . . ." Mack felt bad for her.

"Really Mack, it's fine, I understand. It's better this way if she thinks I'm Miri. She doesn't notice that I have a different voice. It seems that for many, a person's speaking voice tends to fade from memory, but their spoken words still remain."

Mack went in as his mother picked up a large serving tray.

"Aw, Ma. You didn't have to. Here, please let me help you with that." Mack rushed over to take the tray from her. It had three cups of hot tea, along with saucers containing two cookies each, plus a whole box of cookies.

Here I thought she was just getting a box of cookies. Had she dropped this, she could have been scalded! Mack realized.

"These were your favorite cookies growing up, and you always liked peppermint tea." She then leaned over and held her head for a moment, appearing to start to lose her balance.

"Are you okay Ma?" Mack asked with concern.

"I'm fine don't worry about me. But I started getting these awful headaches, since just before I moved here. Because of that, Barry thought I should be taken care of, sweet boy. So, he arranged to bring me here instead of being in our big old house."

"Did you take anything for the headaches?" Mack asked.

"No, never. You know I don't like taking medicines."

"How long have you had them? It could be important."

"Oh, I moved here, just, last week? Didn't I?" She put her hand up to her mouth looking worried and confused, and her voice became shaky. "I can't remember exactly. I just know sometimes my head throbs and I get very weak. But enough about me, I don't like to complain." Betty overheard their whole conversation with her enhanced hearing.

"Now, let me come in and look at you both. You look so good, so healthy! And both so in love, just as I remember." Mrs. Schwartz smiled at them, her eyes sparkling with happiness.

Mack set the tray down and they sat. Mack said a blessing on a cookie took a bite, then did the same for his tea and drank.

"My dear Miri. You aren't having anything. They are kosher after all! I know Barry doesn't care much about that lately, but these cookies and tea are perfectly kosher."

Mack suddenly realized that of course Betty wouldn't eat or drink. He was so used to being with her and eating in front of her that he didn't give it a second thought.

"Ma, she's on a special diet and can't have them, that's all. It has nothing to do with their not being kosher." Mack was now saying Betty's typical line she said to her patients.

"I'm so sorry Mrs. Schwartz, I should have said something beforehand. I didn't mean to put you to any trouble," Betty apologized.

"Now Miri, you know you can call me 'Ma' just like Mack does. You always were so formal!" She chuckled.

"Okay, Ma." Betty smiled at her lovingly.

Mrs. Schwartz started reminiscing now. Her memory

was pretty good today. "I have a photo album here of you two. Do you remember your wedding, and how Mack tried so hard to break the glass?" She started laughing.

Betty did some quick research in her mind:

"Jewish Weddings": At the end of the wedding ceremony, the groom typically wraps a wine or other glass in a napkin or cloth, and proceeds to stomp on it to break it, and then everyone yells "Mazal Tov!"

Betty suddenly snapped out of her research mode as she heard Mrs. Schwartz's voice, seemingly in the distance.

"Miri are you okay?" she asked, concerned about saying something wrong. She didn't want to embarrass them.

"I'm fine, Ma." Betty nodded. "I was just thinking."

"Really, I thought it was a precious moment. Maccabee trying so hard to get that stubborn old glass to break. And he finally got it to! I had always attributed his determination to break that glass, with his love for you." She patted Betty's leg.

Mack smiled and laughed. "I really did try very hard. I was starting to worry that it might not break at all. Oh well, at least I did remember to bring the ring." He pointed at Betty's hand. She held it up, displaying the ring on her finger.

"Here, I will finish the cookies and tea you gave her." Mack ate and drank, then said his blessings for having had them.

They talked and reminisced some more, then there was a knock at the door. Barry came in. "Hi Ma, how are you today?"

"Barel, look who's here! Mack and Miri. I'm so thrilled! You're all here to visit me at the same time!" Mrs. Schwartz was elated; her whole family was here together with her.

Barry came over and hugged Mack, patting him hard on his back. "Hey, how are you, Little Mack? Long time, no see!" Then Betty stood up to come over to meet him, not thinking about the fact that she looked just like Miri.

Barry just stared at her as though he'd seen a ghost much the way Mack did when he first looked at Betty the first time.

"Miriam? But I thought you were, um, dead?" He had no idea how to put it in an elegant way. "I must have gotten you confused with someone else." His mother hadn't heard the comment. She had already left to get more cookies and tea.

"Trust me Barry, it's a long and complicated story." Mack looked at Betty as if to ask permission to tell it over.

"Maybe later, Barry replied. "I've got to get going, but thought I'd drop in for a few minutes to check on Ma and see how she's doing. Looks like she's having a very good day. Nice to see you, um, Miri." Barry still stared at her, wondering how he could get a fact like thinking she was dead, so wrong.

"Bye Ma!" Barry popped his head in to say goodbye.

"Barel, aren't you going to stay? I was making you some tea and we can all sit down together and catch up." Liora looked a bit disappointed as she exited the kitchenette, realizing Barry had already said his goodbyes and left.

Chapter 3
Dr. Betty's Diagnosis

Betty excused herself, got up, then hurriedly left out the door. She went running down the hallway after Barry.

"Barry, please wait up, I need to talk to you a minute!" It appeared to onlookers that Betty ran unusually fast. She was dodging nurses and residents dexterously as she went, her processors accelerating, so that all of humanity seemed as if they were in slow motion to her. She finally caught up with Barry, who was almost ready to exit the building.

"Barry, hey! I need to talk to you. Do you have a minute?"

"How'd you get here so fast? And you don't even appear to be winded!" Barry said rather shocked.

As she came closer to him, she decided to turn up the volume of her recorded breathing pattern to make it more audible, because he was right! That was normal for living, breathing humans. It was something she didn't usually think of to do.

"Listen, about your mother. When did she start to experience her headaches?" Betty asked, now sounding more out of breath.

I will have to remember to eventually turn down the volume of the breathing pattern, she thought.

"She started having them about, um . . . three years ago? It was a year before I brought her here. She started exhibiting signs of dementia, I am not certain whether it was before or after she started having headaches. She doesn't talk much about things that bother her. Why?" Barry seemed puzzled.

"Aside from headaches, did she experience weakness or fatigue? Who diagnosed her?" Betty looked concerned.

"Well, um, she was sixty-six at the time. Sometimes she forgot who I was, and even more so Mack. She started forgetting where she put things, what words to use, couldn't concentrate. She seemed weaker and lost all concept of time. Isn't that kind of normal for dementia and Alzheimer's at that age?" Barry never answered Betty's question, and his micro-expressions told her he wasn't telling the whole story.

"Did anyone diagnose her with dementia when she got here?" Betty pressed the issue.

"Probably. I really don't know. I was just trying to find a place that would take care of her properly. She's my mother, you know? I don't have the time or resources to look after her. I'm out on the road a lot, being a trucker. I did the best that I could for her." Barry found her questioning odd.

"Listen, aren't you just a legal assistant for Mack? I mean, you don't show up for like, over three years, and then suddenly you're so interested in the welfare of my mother? Something doesn't add up. Are you accusing me of not taking care of her properly?" He started getting upset.

"No Barry, not at all. During the last few years, I have worked as a medical caregiver, and I've learned a lot about many different medical conditions. I have reason to believe your mother has quite possibly been misdiagnosed. I was thinking how some medications can lead to dementia, but your mother hasn't ever taken anything. Alzheimer's is a slowly deteriorating brain disease that is ongoing. Dementia is a group of multiple symptoms, which affects brain function. Her headaches make me think it's something else entirely. She does not seem to be deteriorating rapidly. She's still serving tea and cookies and has control of her kitchenette. Most dementia patients would need someone else to do that for them by now."

Barry finally calmed down at her explanation. "So, what do you propose? She has limited insurance coverage, and I sold her house to help pay for her care here."

"If what I suspect is correct, I think she may have a brain tumor, and it would be worthwhile to get her brain scanned. She doesn't like to complain, does she?" Betty asked.

Barry shook his head vigorously. "No-ho-ho. She rarely lets on to anyone when something is wrong. I had to piece together what I know. She would rather suffer than complain. If she seeks help for something, you know it must be bad."

"Let me contact some people I know. They may be able to help. I suspect they may even pay for everything. Thank you, Barry. You have been a great help!" Betty smiled at him.

"Well, okay good. I hope so. I'll try to keep in touch, but as I said, I am on the road a lot. I'd appreciate it if you'd let me know what you find out. Bye Miri," Barry said, looking rather relieved as he went out the door.

Betty walked back to Mrs. Schwartz's room and knocked on the door before entering, as it seemed to be the custom.

"Where have you been?" Mack wondered aloud. "I was beginning to think you ran off with Barry!" he said teasingly.

"Oh Mack, she'd never do that." Mrs. Schwartz smiled.

"I did have a long talk with Barry. I may have some news for you Mack." Betty wasn't sure if she should say anything in front of his mother and didn't want to embarrass her.

"Let me take your used dishes. I'll go put them in the sink." Mrs. Schwartz collected them and went to the kitchen.

"Perfect timing!" Betty was all excited.

"What in the world did you two talk about?" Mack asked.

"I believe your mother has been misdiagnosed. I think she has a brain tumor, not dementia. If what I suspect is correct, it may be operable. If so, all her symptoms could possibly be reversed, and she could go back to normal!" Betty beamed. "I think we should take her to Caring Corp. and see if we can get her an MRI or CT scan. I'm almost certain of it, Mack!"

"Wow, that would be incredible Betty! Would the Kerrings do that for us?" Mack asked. She nodded yes emphatically.

"Do what, and who is Betty? Miri; are you're going by your middle name now?" The comments confused her, but it was surprising she even remembered a form of Miri's middle name.

Mack tried to contain his excitement. "Ma? We want to take you for a checkup. Is that okay? We think there's something the doctors may have missed."

"Okay Maccabee. If it makes you happy. But I don't want to trouble anyone. I feel okay, except for my headaches."

Betty contacted Robert with her mind, and he answered.

"Robbie! Can I ask you a favor? I think that Mack's mom may just have a brain tumor instead of dementia. I believe she has been misdiagnosed. Unfortunately, they don't have much money and the insurance may not cover it, since it is just my own hunch from the things I have learned. Could we get her in and get her scanned?" Betty sat silently staring into space as she did whenever she researched, called or texted in her mind.

"Of course we can get her in. I'll talk to Dad. We would do anything for you and Mack," Robert replied.

"Mack, is Miri okay, it appears that she needs a checkup far worse than I do." Mrs. Schwartz waved her hands over Betty's staring eyes, and she didn't so much as blink.

Mack tried to keep a straight face, between the potential good news and knowing exactly what Betty was doing.

"She's fine Ma, just in very deep thought. She does this now and then. I'm used to it." Mack cracked a smile.

"Thank you, Robbie! Tomorrow morning at 9 a.m.!"

Once her call was finished, Betty suddenly realized that everyone was staring at her. *Oh well,* she thought. *They're waiting for a response anyway, I will just tell them the news.*

"Robbie said tomorrow at 9 a.m.!" Betty said excitedly.

"Did I miss something?" Poor Mrs. Schwartz didn't know what to make of it all.

"It's okay Ma. Bet, uh, Miri made an appointment for a checkup for you at her relative's office." Mack patted his mother's hand. "I think everything may just be okay."

Mack, Betty, and Mrs. Schwartz flew to Albany together on the usual flight and overnighted at Mack's apartment.

Mack explained to his mother that they were certain there was a very fixable problem connected with her health, but she needed a scan to make sure. They arrived at Caring Corp. in Mack's autonomous car. His mother was fascinated. She hadn't been in a robocar before. The Kerrings arranged for the scans to be done, and Mrs. Schwartz was top priority. The best technicians were called in and the scans were done.

Dr. Kerring called Betty to come look at the results.

"Sweetie, you were right! Look at this, it is a classic frontal meningioma, totally benign and operable. That is what has been causing all her headaches and memory loss.

"I knew it!" Betty did some happy victory gestures.

"Are you sure you don't want to become a doctor and work with us?" Dr. Kerring raised his eyebrows and smiled.

"Thanks, but no. I really like working with Mack." Betty smiled and gave him a hug. "How do we proceed?"

"Let's check your mother-in-law into the Cancer Wing and get her scheduled. Does she have any idea what is going on?" Dr. Kerring thought she should at least be informed.

Betty poked her cheek with her finger in thought. "She doesn't know the full story. I'm not sure how to tell her. Let's go ask Mack. He might know what is best. I only first met her yesterday. She and Mack's brother both think I'm Miri."

Betty came running out of the scanning area to the waiting room where Mack was sitting. She jumped up and down, clasping her hands together and had a huge smile.

"Good news I take it?" He laughed at her antics.

"Excellent news Mack! It's just as I suspected. The Kerrings think I should be a doctor now." Betty giggled.

"Whatever would make you happy Betty, but I do like working with you." Mack looked her in her eyes and smiled.

"That was just what I told them. But yes, it is a brain tumor in the frontal lobe. It is benign and totally operable. They can perform a craniotomy, and Ma should hopefully return to her old self within a few weeks. The Kerrings are calling in the best neurosurgeon they know," Betty said excitedly. "But what should we tell your mother?"

Mack said, "I think we should tell her the truth, gently. Let me handle it. I'll put it in a way she can understand."

Mack went into his mother's room and sat beside her.

"Maccabee. What am I still doing here? I need to get

home before your father and Barel start to wonder where I am.”

“Ma, Dad won’t be worried, and we called Barry to let him know what’s going on. You need to know that you have been very sick. You know how you get those bad headaches?”

“Uh-huh, my head hurts right now!” She rubbed it.

“We found the cause of the bad headaches. It requires surgery, but once the operation is done, you shouldn’t be getting any more headaches at all.” Mack held her hand and she was comforted.

The surgery was scheduled for the next day. It went well, and they removed a 3-inch tumor. Mrs. Schwartz was in the recovery room, and Mack brought her a pretty scarf to cover her bandaged, now-shaven head. Even though she was a widow, most married Orthodox Jewish women covered their heads, as was the custom. She preferred scarves and snoods over wigs because she thought they were more comfortable.

She was released a few days later and went back to Des Moines to recover. Kathy and everyone welcomed her back home.

Barry came over to Betty upon their arrival and said, “Miri, I can’t thank you enough. You will have given us our mother back! That is such a priceless gift!” Betty smiled, recalling her comment of wanting to repay Mack. Although she already had something else very specific in mind.

They took extra good care of Mrs. Schwartz at the nursing home, and her recovery was remarkable. She eventually became fully aware and back to her old self.

<h1 style="text-align:center">Chapter 4</h1>
<h2 style="text-align:center">Betty's Future Plans</h2>

One day when Mack had flown to Des Moines and was out, Betty went to visit the Kerrings at Caring Corp. She took an autonomous robotaxi to get there on her own. Most models preferred to use robocars or robotaxis for longer distance transportation, or they got around locally using golf carts at the Caring Corp. facilities.

"Robbie!" It was the standard greeting Betty gave to Dr. Robert Kerring, and of course consisted of her running over to him and picking him up as she hugged him, then swinging him around in a circle.

"Hi, Sis!" Robert laughed as she put him down. "How is your mother-in-law doing?"

"She is doing great, Robbie! We are so pleased. She's like a whole new person. Well, at least to me anyway. To Mack, she's his same old mother. It is so nice to see them interact. She now remembers pretty much everything, but apparently has still blocked out the event of Miri's death."

"It is fairly common for people to block out tragedies Betty. It's the brain's defense mechanism of sorts. So, she still sees you as Miri?" Robert gave her a sad look.

Betty sighed to herself. "Oh, I'm pretty used to it now, kind of living in her shadow. She was a wonderful person, but I need to make a new future of my own. About that. I wanted to ask you some questions. Now please be honest with me." Betty looked at him very seriously.

"You know we are always honest with you Betty. What's up?" Robert asked.

"How different am I from the G-3s?" Betty cocked her head as she often did when she was curious about something.

"They're not all that much different. The G-4 model brains were slightly upgraded from G-3s." Robert smiled and clarified, "Of course, your brain is extremely enhanced, and you are completely unique, but that is beside the point."

Betty shook her head. "I don't mean brain-wise. And of course, I know they all look identical. But aside from the surrogate models not having legs and being mobile, do they have any differences in hardware and physical frames?"

"Well," Robert thought hard about it, stroking his chin. "To answer your question, aside from the legs and faces, the G-3s maybe have slightly less strength to their frames, but they are essentially from the same mold. G-3 models originally were mobile and had legs. When they didn't go over well with the patients, we decided to repurpose them. Then we started the Surrogate Division in the Fertility Center."

Betty looked at him with excitement as he continued.

"It was perfect timing, because Artificial Amnion and Placenta Technology or AAPT was available, and we had created the ectogenesis pods that would be used within the surrogate models. We determined that the need of G-3s to have mobility was not necessary, and that having and even powering the legs was a waste of potential resources. That energy could be better utilized elsewhere in the vital fetal systems. We recycled all G-3 legs into you and the other G-4s, until we started making new ones."

"Eewww!" Betty started kicking her legs and looking at them. "I have someone else's old used legs?"

"You're so funny, Betty! Don't worry, it's only the inner parts, such as the skeletal framework, microcontrollers, and other components that were recycled. Your semi-organic living skin is all your own." He laughed at her kicking antics.

"So, Robbie, here is my question," she said as she stopped her kicking.

"Do I have the capability of being a surrogate just like the G-3 models?" She cocked her head again and looked at him very intently.

Robert frowned in deep thought, again stroking his chin.

"The ectogenesis pods were designed to fit right into place, so that part is actually no different. They are accessible through a large flap on their abdomens. We were originally going to have the filtration and nutrient system tanks located in the back, but since they sat on top of hollow stands, we opted to keep the tanks external and they sat underneath in the stands for easier accessibility. But we originally created them to fit in there."

He gave her a strange look. "But essentially yes, Betty. Physically, you could be a surrogate, although you would experience a heavier load on your resources and would likely have to charge and sleep much more often. A charge may last only four to six hours as opposed to twelve to eighteen. Why Betty, what in the world are you getting at?"

"Do you remember when we were in the courtroom after I won my official personhood, and your father came over and we were talking? He said he thought he recognized Mack from the early days of the Fertility Center."

Robert thought a moment. "Now that you mention it, yes, I do remember him saying that. I'm surprised he wouldn't remember Miriam who your face was patterned from, but I'd imagine Dad only sees you, replacing her with you in his mind. Guaranteed, we are two people who will never see you as Miri." He chuckled. "You're very special to us after all."

Betty smiled slyly. "Well, after he said that, I did a bit of researching into the Caring Corp. Fertility Center's case files."

"Betty, did you hack into our database?" Robert winced. "That's illegal! You can't tell anyone any information you have read on any of the patients. There are HIPAA laws. We could be sued for having a data breach!" he whispered.

"Hack? I'm only connected to the entire Caring Corp. system! Robbie, you know me, I would never tell anybody anything. But I had to see for myself what your father was talking about. My curiosity just tends to get the best of me!"

"I certainly know that for a fact!" He laughed.

Betty was thoroughly excited now. "He also said he thought Mack and his late wife had tried to produce some in vitro embryos. Guess what Robbie, I discovered something!"

"Okay, go on?" He had a worried look on his face.

"Mack and his wife Miri, they didn't just try to create some embryos, they succeeded! They are being stored right here in the Caring Corp. cryopreservation rooms! As best I can estimate, shortly after they were created, Mack was in the accident and Miri died. The embryos have just been sitting there all these years." Betty had a huge smile.

"Betty? What are you thinking?" He shook his finger at her in jest. "I know that look when you're planning to do something, or you've already done something that is a little, well . . . questionable!" He looked at her with one eyebrow raised and crossed his arms.

"Robbie, you know how grateful I am that Mack gained my freedom. I would do anything for him, I love him so very much! I just reasoned that, he and Miri must have wanted to have children very badly. So much so, that they came to the Fertility Center, and for whatever reason that they couldn't have children. Those sweet little embryos are just sitting there frozen with nobody to care for them or raise them. What if I could give Mack as precious of a gift as he gave to me with my freedom?" She had her irresistible expression that nobody could ever stay mad at.

Robert sighed. It was very hard to out-reason or argue with her. "Betty, have you discussed any of this with Mack?"

"No. It is one of those areas where he gets a whole lot of micro-expressions almost all at once that tells me to not go there. We do not talk about children, his plans for them, past, present, or future. I think it hurts him to think of it, knowing that he would never again have Miri, or even the potential to have children anymore since his accident."

"You're probably quite right," He looked down sadly, feeling bad for Mack.

"That's why, I thought of the most perfect idea! . . . Robert?"

He knew she was very serious when she didn't refer to him with her pet name of "Robbie."

"I know what you are thinking Betty. You want to be like a G-3, only still having your legs and mobility." He slightly rolled his eyes, knowing that she usually got her way.

"Yes Robbie, could you please do that for me? "Please, oh please, oh please?" she begged, clasping her hands together.

Robert looked her right in her eyes. "You would tell Mack about this right? I mean, you wouldn't go and carry a baby for nine months and then suddenly say, 'Surprise! I'm having your baby. Here it is!'"

"Well, eventually. After we made sure that they were

completely healthy and doing okay. I wouldn't want to get his hopes up if anything did go wrong for some reason."

Her argument was logical as always. She had no intention of letting Mack feel the pain of losing anyone else.

"Very true Betty. Indeed, you are a wonderful wife. I'm sure you will make an excellent mother too." Robert smiled.

"So, you'll actually help me do it?" Betty was ecstatic.

"I am not promising anything, yet. I may help you do it." He then rubbed his face and eyes and said, "You do know what happened the last time I ended up doing something like that right? I know it was my fault, my initiative to start with, but you became enhanced and then you tweaked yourself and got all emotional. Dad was not very happy with me."

"Just so that doesn't happen again, we should really tell him what is going on. Please?" Robert said with a pleading look on his face. "I'd need help to do the procedure anyway."

"Okay Robbie! Anything to be able to get my babies!" She squealed with delight and again picked him up hugging him and twirling him around.

"Wait, babies, plural? Or do you just mean a baby? Put me down Betty!" Robert knew that she was quite literal at times, and feared what she might really mean.

She put him down, grabbed his arms and stared into his eyes directly, "I saw in the Fertility Center database, there are two embryos. They were listed as one male and one female. I want to have twin babies, Robbie!" Betty beamed.

"Betty, Sis. You aren't even used to carrying one single fetus, let alone two!"

"But the surrogate G-3s have been known to carry twins, haven't they? Not enough room for triplets perhaps, but I know that they have had twins. So could I!" she said proudly.

"You are really serious about this aren't you!" He held her arms as well. Betty nodded affirmatively.

"Let me talk to Dad about the possibilities. I know secretly, he'd love to be a grandparent. I'm always too involved with work and haven't really tried to find the right person yet. I guess, time is cruel and eventually runs out for women. I should probably start thinking about it myself."

Indeed, it was true. Robert wouldn't be young forever.

"Maybe you could have someone in mind for me like you did for Tom and Meg? You are a great matchmaker."

He grinned and took a deep breath, closing his eyes. "Alright Betty. Yes, I will help you."

Betty again squealed and picked him up, while hugging him and twirling him around in circles.

"Sis, I love you, but you're making me dizzy!"

Betty set him down again and tried to calm herself.

"But!" Robert pointed a warning finger. "You are going to have to make some life modifications. Remember, you will be carrying two human lives inside of you. It's not something to be taken lightly, it is serious! You don't want anything to go wrong." He shook his head. "I can't believe I'm doing this!"

Betty sat down, leaned toward him, and listened intently.

"That means, you'll need to charge much more often when you start to get tired and run low on energy. Take many charging naps throughout the day, especially during the third trimester. Most human women have that same issue when they are pregnant too, and they also need to take naps."

"Ideally, you could have the same openable stomach flap as the G-3s for easy access, but wait, that might not even be necessary!" He thought some more, pacing back and forth.

"We can install a visual monitor, and you can do your own ultrasounds periodically. You could even save the images and then Mack could get to see them. You will need to have some new programming installed for monitoring temperature and the children's heartbeats, software to monitor and equipment to run the filtration and nutrient systems. Those circulate using small tubes. Maybe I should have given you that belly button after all." He chuckled. "Now, when are you going to tell Mack?"

Betty thought hard before replying. She knew he was right, and she would have to tell him some time.

"I didn't understand all the things in it, but I remember reading something in one of the volumes of Mack's books called the "Talmud". It basically said that a baby gets its soul after forty days, which would seem to indicate that it is an actual human being at that point. That works out to be 5.71 weeks. If everything has gone well by that time, I can tell him then. It's like at that point, they are officially human!"

"I don't know about the soul part, but for sure, around that time, at about five to six weeks, a human fetus starts to develop brain activity," Robert confirmed.

"Wait, I hear your father coming," Betty exclaimed.

"Oh boy!" Robert braced himself for potential arguments.

"Sweetie! You came to visit us, how nice!" Dr. Kerring gave her a big hug and she hugged him back. "Oh, you must be very excited, because you are kind of hurting me, Betty."

"Oh, I'm sorry Dr. Kerring. Yes, I'm very excited. We have something to discuss with you," Betty said cheerfully.

"Uh-oh, what is it this time?" he said fearfully.

"Dad?" Robert warned, "You better sit down for this one."

"Why, what are you two up to now?" He warily sat down.

"How would you like to be a grandpa?" Betty grinned.

"From which one of you two?" He raised his eyebrows in surprise, wagging his finger back and forth between them.

"Me!" Betty replied. "What's your schedule look like?"

"Is Monday morning at 8 a.m. okay?" she asked. "We have a procedure to perform!"

Betty and Robert reviewed everything with Dr. Kerring that they had discussed before he came in. Much to their surprise, he reluctantly nodded yes, slightly smiling.

Chapter 5
The Procedure

Monday morning, a very cheerful Betty made sure Mack was ready and on schedule to catch his flight for Des Moines. It helped that he had gotten a new case there. Being somewhat complex, it required extra attention. Fortunately for Betty, his concentration was more focused on the details of the case, than on noticing her unusual, happier-than-normal mood.

After she saw him off, Betty rushed in a robotaxi to get to Caring Corp. The doctors were there ready and waiting for her, as she elegantly glided through the automatic doors.

"I'm here!" She could barely contain her excitement.

"Okay, up on the table you go," Robert said to Betty.

"We have a whole lot of work to do today. First, I'll add the G-3 programming for amnionic fluid filtration, monitoring the combined oxygenating and nutrient systems, and the regulation of the pod's temperature. Inside the pod are tiny pump and filtration mechanisms controlled by the new software. As promised, I'll also install the scanning program enabling you to do internal ultrasounds periodically."

He smoothed her hair back over her head, lifted the gasket below her hairline, and plugged the connector into her port.

"The transfer will only take a few minutes. Your operating system is backward compatible, so it will readily accept the G-3 programming," Robert stated with confidence.

"Were the embryos thawed and prepared?" she asked.

"Yes Betty," Dr. Kerring replied. "We have the cultured endometrial tissue medium already in place within the pod. The embryos implanted into it successfully. Right now, the pod is temporarily hooked up to filtration and nutrient supply systems. I must say Betty, they are looking great!"

"Okay, program installations are complete. Disconnecting now." Robert sealed her gasket and put her hair back down.

"We are ready! Are you sure you want to do this Betty? We have two available G-3s ready on standby just in case you changed your mind." Robert looked at her questioningly.

"I'm so very sure Robbie!" She got off the table to hug him.

Betty looked over at Dr. Kerring who said, "Oh Betty, just call me 'Dad.' We all know that's what I am to you. Besides, it may seem odd to your children if you call me 'Dr. Kerring.'"

"Thank you, Dad!" Betty hugged and picked him up to twirl him around as he smiled. After she put him down, Dr. Kerring started looking over Robert's diagrams. He was visibly impressed.

"You should come once a week for filtration and nutrient care," Dr. Kerring advised. Betty nodded that she understood.

"Looks like Robert designed it so that . . . no!" He stared closer at one of the diagrams then looked at Betty and laughed. "You'll have two 'belly buttons.' Very funny!"

He thought it was cute how close Betty and Robert were.

The two had always joked about her lack of a belly button.

Robert explained, "There are two tubal connectors. The top fitting is the nutrient supply with inner female threads. The bottom fitting has outer male threads connecting to the filtration system to drain wastes. Each is capped when not in use."

Dr. Kerring confirmed, "Normally those are not visible, since G-3s have them coming up from their bases into their bodies with access from the stands below. Since you said you didn't want a stomach flap, that would be a logical choice."

"Okay Sweetie, do you want to be awake or asleep for this?"

"I want to be awake and watch everything!" Betty said.

"Alright. I kind of figured you would. Okay, let's bring the team in here and get everything started," Dr. Kerring said as he went to wash his hands and put on some latex gloves.

They sterilized the area and made a U-shaped incision from one side of her tummy to the other. They peeled her organic living skin and capacitive sensor layer back, and cut the webbed heating elements, capping the ends to prevent shorting. It still retained power to heat to normal body temperature, so they put the webbing back and over the skin to keep it warm.

Betty watched everything in fascination as it took place. Robert installed an emergency transmitter beacon, just in case anything ever went wrong, and she couldn't reach him. That way, if for some reason Betty was out of commission, it would send a notice immediately so the babies could be located and rescued.

Everything was planned out meticulously, since a mobile model had never been a surrogate before. All precautions that could be taken were implemented to protect the lives of the two human fetuses that would be growing inside of Betty. Robert installed a reserve backup battery, and a special monitor to sense increased fetal activity, alerting her in advance of the proper extraction time.

"The abdominal ultrasound scanning device can be placed in the back. It's the reverse of normal but should work just the same for your purpose. Then you can visually keep tabs on the fetuses as they grow and send the pictures to the cloud to share with Mack if he wants to see them." Robert talked as he worked, connecting and putting all the equipment in place.

Next, the small filtration and nutrient tanks were installed in the back toward the bottom of her abdominal cavity, one on either side, where human kidneys would normally be located.

Now, they were ready for the last and final element! The team brought over the ectogenesis pod containing the now thawed and living male and female embryos. It's supporting frame snapped right into place, attaching directly to Betty's skeletal system. The filtration and nutrient tanks were then connected to the pod, and two small tubes came out toward the front for connection at the "belly buttons" to enable draining and filling. The webbed heating elements floated freely atop the pod, and the tubes were fed between the webbing.

The living cultured skin cell tissue layer was carefully

placed over the pod. Two small incisions were made for the tiny tubal fittings to come out lower to mid-belly. All incisions were coated with cellular bonding paste, and sheets of cultured skin cell tissue were placed on top all along the absorbable sutures.

Betty was bandaged up for protection. Her skin would be sealed, healed and waterproofed within forty-eight hours, and no scars would remain. She activated her new programming, tested it, and all functions were running successfully.

"Congratulations!" Everyone in the room from caregiver model assistants to humans were celebrating yet another major life event for Betty. She was now the first ever, mobile G-4 caregiver model to officially be "pregnant."

"Just take it easy for the next two days as you heal and be sure to get extra sleep and charging. You may not notice much difference in power usage at first. The filtration and nutrient flow regulation is very minimal when the fetuses are small."

Dr. Kerring stroked his stubbly beard in thought. He just kind of smiled and stared at Betty with a contented look.

Robert chimed in, "By the third trimester, you'll really be working hard to keep up with the needs of all three of you. I'd recommend taking a charging nap every four hours."

"Sweetie? I know you may feel a bit tacky from the cellular bonding paste, but please don't take any showers until after two days. You basically had the equivalent of major surgery for a human, so it may even take a little longer than normal to heal." Dr. Kerring hugged her ever so gently.

"Robert is right. You are going to make a spectacular mother!" He winked at her and smiled. "I do feel a bit guilty about not informing Mack, and your decision to surprise him with this. Does he deal with surprises well? You would know him better than I do," Dr. Kerring asked hesitantly.

"Well, he tried to surprise me when he proposed, so I would think he's okay with surprises himself," she reasoned. "I'm so happy and excited! This is the most priceless gift I could ever give him, even more than his mother being back to her old self. I had already thought of this before. My 'heart' was set on it."

"Notice: Power now at 35 percent," went the warnings inside her head. "Whew, I am feeling a little tired. I think I should go lie down and charge a while before I leave."

"Excellent idea Sweetie. You've been through a lot. Your processors are likely taxed to their limits with all the newly added programming." Dr. Kerring escorted her to a nearby charging bed. He removed her gasket and plugged her in.

"Thank you, Dad, for everything!" She smiled sweetly.

"Oh Sis," Robert called out then came over next to her.

"Next time you come to visit, please don't be picking us up and twirling us around. You could accidentally pull something vital inside of you or dislocate it. It could be extremely dangerous for the babies. Now, I'm very serious Betty."

"Okay Robbie, you're absolutely right. I know I need to

be much more careful from now on," Betty agreed with him.

"Oh gosh. I hope I can keep a straight face around Mack if he comes by before you tell him the news. I'm not great with surprising people or keeping news from them. I really hope you know what you're doing Sis." Robert sighed.

Dr. Kerring left for a bit, and Betty charged for four hours.

"Mack arrives at home in a little over an hour, so I need to get going. It is unusual for a direct charge to take so long."

"While I've got you here, Sis . . ." Robert couldn't resist trying to find the special coding that gave Betty emotions. He plugged her into a laptop and copied all her coding into a file to examine later. He disconnected her diagnostic port.

Dr. Kerring returned just in time to see Betty off.

"Good luck, Sweetie, I'm sure Mack will be thrilled when he finds out!" He gently hugged her, afraid to put pressure on the ectogenesis pod. Indeed, he would be a doting grandpa.

"Thank you, Dad," Betty smiled at him lovingly. She kissed a busy Robert on the cheek as she left to go home.

Robert started doing a comparative analysis between the adjusted coding he had programmed into Betty four years earlier, and what she had added. He was looking through the series of 1s and 0s for anomalies, when very specific sets of As, Cs, Gs and Ts suddenly went across the screen. Then, a popup appeared, and flashed a warning, "Forbidden! Access denied!"

That piqued his interest. He jotted down the letters with

a pen on a paper. He tried running it again with the same result. Each time, he wrote down more letters, then the screen flashed the same warning. By the sixth attempt, Robert saw the message change. On the seventh try, the screen displayed zigzagging lines and the laptop overheated. The screen cracked and the casing caught fire. Smoke detectors went off, and he quickly ran to get a nearby fire extinguisher.

Dr. Kerring came running in, "What on earth happened Robert? Are you alright? What did you do this time?"

"It was the most curious thing, Dad. I was trying to isolate Betty's special code to see what makes up her emotions. Instead of 1s and 0s, there were letters. I've never seen anything like it!" He scratched his head, then picked up his notes to show his father. "Letters A, C, G and T in specific combinations?"

Dr. Kerring looked at the singed paper in Robert's hand and said, "That's basic DNA Robert. I think you've discovered Betty's secret." Dr. Kerring looked at Robert, and back at the dead computer with half fear, half wonderment. The laptop was totally inoperable, and all access to the code was lost.

"Unless I totally imagined it, before the last message, I thought I saw, 'Stop! This cannot be accessed,'" Robert added.

Dr. Kerring sternly looked his son in the eyes, saying, "Robert? Either your subconscious was sending you a message, or the fumes of the overheating laptop got to you. You need to stop experimenting with Betty's code. Enough! No more!"

Chapter 6
Melissa's Plot

About two months after Jimmy's incarceration, Melissa finally came to visit him at the minimum-security prison. She still hadn't gotten the bank password from him. That was the last thing she needed him for was to gain access to all the money they had embezzled from Quality First Airlines.

"You've got a visitor," the corrections officer called to Jimmy. He was taken to the visitation booth.

"Hey Booboo Bear!" Melissa smiled as Jimmy settled into his chair. "How are they treating you?"

"Okay, I guess. Thanks for coming, Doll. It means a lot. Even my own mother hasn't come. It's like that Bucket of Bolts Betty Bot has ripped my whole life apart!" he snarled.

Melissa looked puzzled. "I knew she was trouble when I first met her. Seemed just too nice to be true. Why did you even hire her? She's manipulated everyone around you to do her bidding. You said in court that you bought that thing?"

"Yeah. It was a bad experiment gone wrong. Enough about Bucket of Bolts. I did everything you asked me to do. When you gonna reward me, Doll? You promised you'd reward me! They do allow conjugal visits here in New York, heh-heh-heh."

Jimmy grinned and put his hand on the glass, and Melissa reciprocated, then put her hand down and got her phone out.

"Soon enough Jimmy. Why didn't you tell me the password before? It would've been so easy." Melissa gestured like a phone, pointed to her ear and then out toward the entrance so he knew they were likely being listened to. She did a gesture pointing to her eyes and his, then out to the room and gave a thumbs up, indicating there were no cameras watching. She took out a piece of gum, started chewing on it, blowing and popping her bubbles.

"I love you, Angel. I was protecting you! If you didn't know it, they couldn't connect you. This way, you weren't involved. No sense in both of us winding up in here," he said with a plaintive look on his face, and again put his hand on the glass.

She just stared at him with a blank look, chewing away.

"You know that day when all the fire alarms went off? Turns out Megan, my traitor of a cousin had snuck up on us and took a video of when we started 'our plans.' " He gestured air quotes. "I think this was all her doing!" he growled with a frown.

"Oh dear, I forgot my email password." She got ready to type on her phone. "Can you please remind me what it is?"

"Gee Melissa, you'd think that's all you cared about."

"Boo, you know I care about you, otherwise I wouldn't be here visiting." She popped a bubble and then kept on chewing.

"What's the password?" she said, with an air of impatience.

"It's the word 'money' in all lowercase, then 1-2-3. Isn't that clever?" He smiled proudly.

"Thank you." Melissa tried typing it in. "I'm in!" She

looked up at him with a huge smile, but as she looked back down at her phone, her face went white, and her jaw dropped. "Jimmy, is this some kind of joke? Where is it?"

"What do you mean 'where is it?'" He frowned.

"It's a big goose-egg!" she yelled, showing him her phone.

"That's impossible! When I was in there last, it was showing over ten mill-aliters!" he said in disbelief.

"Who else had access to this account?" Melissa had her arms crossed, looking at him sternly.

"Nobody Doll, only me!" Unless, well Megan couldn't have. She knew about it, but she never knew how to access the account." Jimmy was thinking hard. "And she wouldn't."

"I want it back right now!" She pounded the table. "How are we going to get it back Jimmy? I might get in serious trubb . . ." Melissa suddenly stopped.

"But it was both of ours, Angel. I thought we were gonna go out and vacation in the Bahamas and do all kinds of stuff like I promised you. Why are you so upset, and whataya mean by you might get in serious trouble?" He looked at her suspiciously.

"Nothing Jimmy. So, what are we going to do? How are we going to get it all back? Any ideas?" She waited for a response.

"There's not much I can do from in here. But maybe . . . ?" Jimmy smiled and frowned at the same time as he thought. "Hmm. A trader for a traitor. The Quality First Fourth of July company picnic is tomorrow evening. Uncle Warbucks has an annual shindig at his place in the country for all the employees."

"Yeah, I remember it last year." Melissa smiled back.

"Uncle Jasper would do just about anything for his only darling daughter, and for sure she'll be there. It might just be a great party to crash." Jimmy winked at her, and she understood exactly what he was getting at.

"I've got to call someone to invite to the party." She winked back. I'm sure he'll tell me just what to do and how to go about doing it. When exactly do you get out of here?" Melissa started to get up out of her seat.

"I was sentenced to five for Bucket of Bolts, and then another three for the company. That's a total of up to eight."

Jimmy suddenly thought a moment. "You are gonna wait for me, aren't you, Angel?"

Melissa spat her gum into the wrapper to throw out. She got up and scooted the chair in, bending over to finish her conversation with him on the visitation booth phone.

"Uh, sorry Jimmy. I have a life to live, and I don't plan on being old and alone. You're much better off to just forget about me. Maybe I'll see you around when you get out. Best of luck in here Jimmy!" She hung up the phone and left.

Her name could be heard echoing throughout the entire prison, as Jimmy screamed after her, "Melissa! Melissa! . . ."

As soon as Melissa got out of the prison from her visit, she called Gio, the man she was working for. Half annoyed and half scared, she had never crossed him before. She had heard from others that you didn't want to get on his bad side.

"Gio?" Melissa was physically trembling.

"Hey Melissa, just the friendly voice I wanted to hear. Did you get that password and withdraw the money as promised? I can't wait to see all that dough!" Gio sounded very enthusiastic.

"Well, yes. I got the password, but there is a problem."

"I don't like problems Melissa," he was sounding upset.

She got edgy. "I'm on my cell and there are people around."

Gio replied, "You know I don't like cellphones, they can be tracked and listened to. Let's meet in person. Come on over to Scarolie's restaurant tomorrow at 5 p.m. I'll be in the private room in the back. It'll be crowded in the front." She agreed.

The next day she arrived right on time at Scarolie's.

"Melissa! Lovely as always." Gio greeted her with a kiss on each cheek, and they sat down at a table. He was a handsome Italian man, relatively young for a gangster.

"I took the liberty of ordering for us. Now tell me exactly what happened." Gio motioned for her to start talking.

A waitress hurried over with his order and brought a large basket of breadsticks with pats of butter, then left.

"I entered the password, but the account was at zero!"

Gio asked, "Did your mark double-cross you? Exactly how much are we talking, Melissa?"

"Ten mil Gio, ten mil!" She was getting upset herself.

"Where'd the money go, and how do we get it back?" Gio said sternly as he started to dig into the luscious food.

"I don't know where the money went, but I don't think it was Jimmy's doing. He seemed genuinely surprised when he heard about it. He's not the brightest person in the world and gets caught up in emotion. He'd make a lousy grifter, you can read him like a book. To tell you the truth, I am so super glad that I can now be rid of him. Oh, man, I couldn't stand that guy!" She crinkled her face, shuddering her shoulders.

"He treated people terribly. I had to put on a big show to make him think that I liked him, but thankfully he bought it. That was a really hard job Gio. It went on forever!"

She started to eat some food but was too nervous, sensing Gio's displeasure that the money was missing. She raised and pointed her fork. "He did have a pretty good idea though." She hoped Jimmy's suggestion would appease him.

"Alright Melissa, I hope so. Because at this point, right now, you're owing me the ten million bucks. And I'm sorry, but I've got a reputation to uphold. I can't let anyone get away with anything, no matter how much I like them. You showed a lot of promise on your first job here, but that's all changed now," he reprimanded her. His voice became more tense and gruff.

"Gio, listen to me, please. Jimmy's got a rich uncle who owns the airline, right? And it was his cousin that ratted him out, so he's got no love for her. She probably got the Feds involved would be my guess. The way I figure it, she or even better her father, owes you the money. Let's kidnap her, hold her for ransom, and ask for the ten mil he owes you. I'm going to need some help with it though. I can't do it alone."

Gio finished sucking up some spaghetti, and wiped his mouth daintily with the corner of a napkin he took off his lap.

"Sounds great. Here, you can use my car, it goes from zero to sixty in 2.5 seconds." He threw her the keys to his classic red 2017 Maccino 240 sports car. "This is a good test for you. Take the cousin, get a bag over her head, tie her up, and bring her over to the warehouse on Central Avenue. I don't care how you do it, just get her there. But don't let her see you. If she can identify you, it's a big problem. Understand?" She nodded.

"I'm trusting you with my favorite car. I'll have one of my drivers come for me with my luxury sedan."

"But Gio, please, I need help! I don't think I can do it all by myself, I'm not strong enough to subdue someone!" Melissa was visibly worried.

"What's the matter Melissa. You're not eating. You don't like the food? Waitress!" he yelled, snapping his fingers and motioning her over. "Could you please get this pretty lady a doggy bag?" She nodded yes and left to get one.

"Thanks Gio. I'll do my best, but really, I do need help."

The normally cool and collected Melissa was secretly terrified inside as to how she was going to pull this job off.

Gio got up as she was leaving and placed his hand on her shoulder very hard whispering, "I've got confidence in you. Don't let me down . . . or you're dead, Sweetheart."

"Hey!" Gio saw a man come in. "Alright Melissa, you're in luck. Someone very special just arrived." Gio smiled and greeted him with a pat on the back. "I think you remember Four-Finger Tony?" Melissa grinned coyly. "He can help you get the cousin."

"How ya doin' Boss? Hey Melissa, good to see you again! So, you gotta job for me Boss?" Tony asked enthusiastically.

"Yeah Tony. Melissa here needs help to nab someone. We're going to hold her for ransom so her rich daddy pays back the money Melissa owes me," Gio replied, as if it were commonplace to kidnap people. But in his world, it was.

"You know the routine, come up from behind, then 'bag, bind and bring, but don't let 'em see a thing!'" Gio reiterated his standard phrase for Melissa's benefit. "Nothing to it. It's easy."

"Right Boss. The usual, 'Bag, Bind 'n' Bring'," Tony remarked. He had clearly done this before. It was a typical two-man operation that all Gio's goons used to capture people, yet not be able to be identified, if at all possible.

"Go get that cousin. . . . Now!" Gio shouted.

Tony and Melissa left in Gio's favorite car, and she drove since she remembered the way to Jasper's country cabin. Melissa had a very good time there the year before at the employee picnic, even though she was there with Jimmy.

Chapter 7
Fourth of July Picnic

The employees of Quality First Airlines and their families flocked to Jasper Coates's annual Fourth of July party at his huge deluxe cabin in the country surrounded by beautiful woods. Even former employees came. They served hot dogs, burgers and even big juicy steaks. Then later in the old farm fields across the dirt road, there would be fireworks displays after dark. It was Jasper's way of showing the employees his appreciation for their hard work, where they could just kick back and relax.

Mack and Betty arrived. Neither of them could eat the food, so they went over to the lawn chairs where Meg and Tom sat.

"Wow, look at all the familiar faces!" Betty remarked as more people started arriving. "Hey, there's Dawn and Gita! I'm going to go over and talk to them if it's okay Mack."

"It's fine with me Betty. You don't need to ask for my permission," Mack reassured her. She looked at him sweetly.

"I brought my laptop; I can sit here and work. You provided plenty of kosher food for me, as always." He smiled at her.

"The drinks in the ice chests were okay, I'll get a bottle of cola or water later." He took off his suit jacket and sat on a chair. He motioned for her to leave. "Go, have fun Dear! I'll be fine."

"Thanks for understanding Mack. It's so nice to be able to socialize. I've rarely been out since the trial, except to go to

Caring Corp. or Des Moines. Maybe enough time has passed that we no longer need to worry about robot-hating protesters."

She ran over to Dawn and Gita and greeted them with a big hug, asking how they were doing, and they said how much they missed her. They introduced Betty to the three older flight attendants Jimmy had laid off. After Jasper fired Jimmy, he rehired all three with the deepest of apologies, and insisted they keep their out-of-court settlements. Jasper was determined to make things right and treat people fairly.

Quality First's original CPA was cleared for health and returned to work. She came to the picnic, as well as the new Chief Human Resources Officer Jasper had hired to replace Jimmy. He was a friend of senior flight attendant Roy Turner's.

Betty saw her friend and old coworker Roy standing over by the grill, so she went over to talk to him.

"Roy, my man!" She ran up to him with her arms in the air and gave him a big hug. "I haven't seen you since the trial! You just kind of disappeared into the crowd. I wanted to invite you to my victory party, but it got so crazy in the courtroom. Then I couldn't find you. I can't thank you enough for being a character witness. It meant so much to me."

"Aw, Betty. Things just aren't the same without you. Nobody gets sick or hijacked anymore!" He laughed, and she gave him a gentle joking punch in the shoulder.

She noticed someone else familiar far off in the distance.

Betty zoomed her vision in on them. It was Melissa and a man!

"So nice to see you Roy, I'll talk to you in a bit. There's something I need to do," Betty said with a faraway look.

"Enjoy the powder room." Roy snickered. "It's really plush in there. The foaming soap smells just heavenly!"

Betty giggled. He had forgotten about the fact that being man-made, she would never need to use a restroom.

Right now, Betty was more concerned about the potential party crashers that had just shown up. She was reasoning it over in her mind: *I don't recognize this guy who's with Melissa. Maybe he is her "plus one" with Jimmy in jail? But why would Jasper even invite her since she was involved in the embezzlement scheme to steal his money? Meg had told me Melissa never came back to work after the trial.*

Betty kept an eye on them. It appeared they had binoculars and avoided the crowd, staying in the shady wooded areas behind trees and bushes. She could see their heat signatures perfectly when she switched to her infrared vision mode.

Very odd that they stay away from people when this is supposed to be a social get-together, Betty thought.

Tom left Meg and Mack to go talk with some other pilots.

"It's a picnic in July, Mack. You didn't need to bring your suit!" Meg razzed him. He loosened his tie and said he was fine.

Meg got a bit bored that Mack wasn't talking and just sat there working on his laptop, so she excused herself to use the restroom. She walked from the front clearing full of chairs and picnic tables to the cabin located in the back of the property; a place of comfort where she'd spent so many childhood summers.

Betty saw that Melissa and the guy were watching Meg, and they started to go toward the cabin after her. Betty tuned her ears toward them and tried to single out and isolate their voices from the crowd and music playing.

Meg finished washing her hands, then went out of the cabin onto the large back porch to simply breath in the fresh country air, gaze at the woods and view her old childhood hangouts, like the treehouse Jasper had lovingly built for her.

Melissa and Tony had gone to the back of the cabin, hoping to enter unnoticed, not thinking that Meg would come back there too. It was even better than they had planned! They went stealthily up and onto the porch, came up behind Meg, and pressed what felt like a gun against her lower back.

"Don't move, don't make a sound. Do exactly as we say, and you won't be hurt," said a whispering voice.

Meg put her arms up, hoping Betty was nearby. She was facing away from them, having been looking out over the porch railing toward the backyard. Melissa got a hood over Meg's head, and Tony secured her wrists with zip ties.

"Please, please don't hurt me. Whatever you need, I'll get it for you!" Meg whimpered beneath the bag.

"You're going to walk over with us and get into a car,"

Melissa ordered her, still whispering. Betty heard them and snuck around to the other side of the cabin to follow them.

Holding his unloaded gun to Meg's head, Tony whispered, "Where did the money go?" and he cocked the trigger.

"What money? I don't have any money with me." She started crying, "Plee-hee-hee-heez, don't hurt me-hee-hee!"

"We won't, if you tell us where that money is!" Melissa was getting frustrated. This blubber puss wasn't telling them anything. She finally raised her voice, "The money you took from Jimmy! Where's the ten million bucks! Tell us now!"

Too terrified to even recognize that it was Melissa, all Meg could think about was Tom and her unborn baby.

"I don't know! My friend Betty dealt with all that. She got the local legal authorities involved to return the money. I don't know anything about it, really. Please, don't do this!"

They partially took off the hood, taped her mouth with duct tape, then Tony put it back over her face, all from behind so as not to be seen. Betty had heard Meg crying, and Tony and Melissa talking with the volume of her hearing turned up.

"Alright, we'll see if your father wants you back alive. He better give us our money back or you're dead," Tony sniped.

They marched Meg along the edge of the property unseen in the shadows over to Gio's car, still sticking Meg in the side with the gun. They propped her against the back bumper.

"Don't move, just sit there. We're going someplace else."

Melissa and Tony got Meg's ankles restrained with zip ties, then dumped her into the trunk of the car and closed the lid.

Thinking Meg could suffocate in the trunk, there was reason to intervene to protect another person from harm. Betty watched as they slowly drove Gio's car that had been parked far away and unnoticed. In the meantime, she called Mack using her computer mind to tell him what was going on. She needed to borrow their car, and he should go home with Tom.

She got in Mack's autonomous robocar and followed Melissa, who drove Gio's sports car very slowly making sure it wouldn't get so much as a scratch. Betty had hacked into the car's GPS system, so she could track it herself as it went. It was the only car Gio owned that had a GPS.

As they drove, Betty talked to Mack's car in her mind as she used to do with machines, *"I doubt there will ever be a time in which every car on the road will be autonomous and electric-powered like you are. The world would be a much safer, cleaner place. But power-hungry humans like the one who owns the car we are following, will always want to be in control of large, gasoline-powered mechanical vehicles. Psychologically, it makes them feel powerful and in-control to drive on their own."*

Mack's car gave no response, so she gathered she was wasting her time communicating complex concepts to it.

They eventually reached a populated area. Betty spoke to Mack's car saying, *"Please go as fast as you legally can."*

It obeyed, and eventually caught up with the sports car, which had gotten stuck at a red light. Melissa then turned on to the highway. Betty had to think fast. How could she intercept the car, without letting Melissa know that she was responsible?

Betty got an idea. Although the car they were following was mechanical, it still had an onboard computer system and electronically controlled parts. Computer etiquette consisted of a handshake protocol. This car's computer was not so easily charmed. She had a rough time getting around firewalls and encryption. Betty and Gio's car had a whole conversation in her mind. It finally allowed her access after logical reasoning, and she tapped into the car's system. It pays to have a computer brain!

Let's see in here, what can I do that will still keep the passengers and other drivers safe, Betty thought. She had the sports car's horn start blaring in random patterns, then she made all the lights start blinking. The car was such a spectacle that other drivers on the highway distanced themselves. Even the autonomous cars had their sensors alerted to stay away.

Now, with all the other cars out of the way, Betty made Gio's car slow down to a crawl, then she started taking control of the steering, making it swerve from side to side.

"What in the . . . ?" Melissa had no idea what was happening, and wondered why she couldn't control the car. *Gio's really going to kill me if I crash his car!* Melissa thought.

Meg felt the car swerving around. She had a glimmer of

hope that it was most likely Betty's doing and stopped crying.

Betty then proceeded to contact the police with her mind.

"9-1-1, what is your emergency?" dispatch answered.

"I'd like to report an unsafe driver, M-A-R-I-N-O-1 is the license plate. They're heading southwest on I-87 South. I saw her kidnap my friend. Please send Highway Patrol at once!"

"I am seeing it on the traffic cams. The motorist is driving very erratically. Reporting it now, Ma'am."

"Please instruct the officers to rescue my friend at the scene. I am following them from a short distance behind in my blue autonomous car, license plate 1-4-1 dash L-A-W. I can drive up, my friend can get out, and then we'll go to the police station to file a report and issue a statement afterward."

"Yes, Ma'am. I will instruct the officers accordingly."

Soon after, a police car came racing to the scene, lights flashing, siren whooping, as the red sports car kept weaving wildly around the highway, all under Betty's careful control.

Melissa was concentrating on trying to be able to drive and saw a cop car coming up on her in the rear-view mirror.

Betty returned the sports car to normal, and Melissa regained control of the steering wheel, just in time to get off of the highway exit ramp and pull over to stop the car at the side of the road.

"License and registration?" the pair of cops yelled.

Melissa told Tony to run, so he took off his seatbelt.

"Officers, I'm so glad to see you, my car was going crazy

all by itself!" Melissa cried. Tony got out of the passenger's side and ran off. Being a cross-country runner, he easily got away. The officers thought he was the victim escaping when he could.

"Yeah, cars can just go crazy on their own. Stop right there Miss!" the male officer shouted, undeterred by Tony's diversion.

The female officer went behind Melissa and took over.

"Place your hands on top of the car," and she pushed her toward the car to frisk her. "No weapons on her," she shouted.

"Now let's go over there and walk a straight line. Touch your finger to your nose." As the lady cop was doing the procedure, the male officer noticed Betty in Mack's robocar now pulling up next to them. It was the car that dispatch had described would come to help. Betty motioned to the officer, pointing at the trunk. Then he realized what had happened and popped the trunk lid.

As the sobriety tests went on, Melissa didn't notice the robocar had pulled up. The male officer cut Meg's zip ties, took the bag and tape off, then helped her out of the trunk. She ran into Betty's arms sobbing. Betty thanked the officer. Melissa saw Meg and Betty as they got in the robocar and drove away.

The officers took Melissa into the station and booked her for attempted kidnapping. They contacted Gio about his car. Upon hearing about her botched job, he feigned ignorance and said his car had been stolen. Melissa ended up in the same prison as Jimmy, but in a separate wing for women only.

Now fearing for her life, Melissa used her one phone call.

"Hi Gio?" This was her only shot at redemption.

"Yes Melissa? Do you have any last words? I told you what happens if I don't get my money," Gio taunted her.

"Please listen Gio. I know what happened to the money now. It was Jimmy's robot, Betty Fourré. She reported it to the legal authorities and got it all returned. This time, Megan, Jimmy's cousin, ratted out her friend Betty the Robochick."

"How do I know I can trust you, Melissa?"

"Listen, I just got arrested for trying to help you get your money back. Please hear me out." She noted his silence.

He realized she couldn't talk openly and let her speak.

"Betty Fourré is considered a national hero. Don't trust me, research it yourself! The whole country would do anything for her. She got a gold medal of honor and is very popular."

"But she can be trouble Gio," Melissa warned him. "Somehow, she hacked in and took control of your car. She very nearly crashed it with me, Tony, and her friend inside."

"But I'm telling you, if you want your dough back, she's where to look. I hope with this info we're even."

"Okay Melissa, if it pans out, we're even. If what you say is true, she may be worth more than ten. Thanks for the tip." Gio hung up.

He did some investigating and found out she was right.

Chapter 8
Announcing the News

Two months had now passed since Betty's procedure had been done. She went to Caring Corp. for testing, and all was fine and in order. All tests passed, and the babies were healthy and doing well inside her ectogenesis pod. Their brain activity even seemed slightly advanced for their age. Betty played classical music to them almost every day and spoke softly to them with her internal speaker. She was a doting mother already. Now, she wanted to give the happy news to Mack that he was going to be a father, to not just one, but two babies!

Mack got home from his flight and collapsed on the living room couch in his apartment. Betty came to greet him, but he had already fallen asleep. She put a blanket over him and tucked him in. She knew he was to stay home tomorrow.

He awoke in the morning, said his morning statement of gratitude upon waking, "Modeh Ani . . ." and opened his eyes to see Betty standing next to him with a huge smile.

"Betty!" He noticed how he had been lovingly tucked in with the blanket. "You take such good care of me. I need to go and say my morning prayers and all. Thank you for everything that you do for me." He smiled and got up to do his morning routines. Betty went in the kitchen and fixed him an extra-special meal. She had it timed perfectly so that when he got back, he would eat breakfast. She could give him the news then.

He said his blessings for his food, and commented how delicious everything was. Betty was unusually quiet, sitting at the table watching him eat, and smiling at him contentedly.

"Betty Dear, are you okay? You're so quiet," he noted.

That was about to change. She was running simulations, processing outcomes of various scenarios as to how to tell him the news, and what his potential reactions would be.

"Mack," she started to tell him.

"Yes, Betty?"

"When is the last time that I thanked you for such a precious gift that you have given me of gaining my freedom?" She smiled sweetly.

"Um, I think it was a couple of days ago, but Betty, you know I would do it all over again in a heartbeat. I am so happy to see you free and thriving." He smiled back at her, and then sipped his cup of coffee.

"Mack?" She interlaced her fingers, stretched out her arms, palms outward, and plopped them on her lap. He saw she wanted to discuss something and looked at her a bit puzzled.

"Are you sure you're alright? You're acting a bit . . . unusual. But you do seem extra happy, even for you."

"What if I could give you as precious of a gift as you gave to me, with my freedom?" She cocked her head in her innocent and irresistible way.

"Freedom is priceless. You can't put a price on it. You owe me nothing Betty, really! You did save my mother, so we're even!"

This isn't going to be as easy as I thought it would be. I have played it through several simulations, but it's not as I pictured. She made a bit of a frowning face as she thought.

"Mack?"

"Betty what is it? You're making me start to worry."

"I have arranged to give you the most priceless gift imaginable. I know you don't talk about it, but I looked into the Caring Corp. Fertility Center records. I saw that you and Miri had two embryos cryopreserved." She grinned at him.

"Mack just kind of stared at her. "Why were you fishing around in my files Betty? That is not very nice. That is ancient history, a part of my life that will never happen. Please don't go there, it is too painful for me. I have my life with you now. I don't need to dwell on the past. Please do not mention it again." He finished his coffee and went into the living room planning to sit on the couch to read.

He looked up, "By the way, thank you for the breakfast, it was delicious." He looked back down. She could tell he was hurting, so she had to tell him the news to cheer him up.

"Mack?" she tried to explain to him again.

"Betty what is it? You're acting very odd this morning!"

"I'm carrying those embryos. You're going to be a father!"

He stood up. She went over to him, but he backed away.

"What did you say?" He looked at her in total disbelief.

"I arranged to have an ectogenesis pod, exactly like the older G-3s. I am now a surrogate. The babies, yours and Miri's babies, are about two months along. You're going to be a father, Mack!" She smiled a huge smile. "Isn't that wonderful news?" Again, she went nearer to him, but he backed away.

"No, no, no!" he said, shaking his head, "This isn't real. I must be dreaming!" He pinched himself and he cried out.

"What have you done? We were so happy together! You found out, and just took the embryos, Miri and my embryos? You had no right! I should have had a say in it and been the one to make that decision. How could you? And the Kerrings? They actually went along with all of this? And without my permission! How could they? I feel . . . very betrayed!"

Mack collected his suitcase and laptop that he had just brought home. He thought about even getting a motel room for the night, just to have a quiet place to think things through.

"Betty, I just need some time to think and process this. I've got to go; I can't stay here right now. When my head is clear, I'll come back. I just need to think about all of this." He left out the door, closing it hard without even saying goodbye.

Betty ran after him and flung the door open. "Mack!" She yelled after him, but he kept going. She then started whimpering uncontrollably as was her way of crying. She held her tummy thinking about the precious babies inside.

"Why? Why is your father being like this!" she said to the babies, then whined and whimpered feeling helpless and alone.

Betty called up Caring Corp. asking for one of the Kerring doctors. Nobody was available now. There had been an accident, and a car crashed into a nearby utility pole causing a major power outage at Caring Corp. One of the backup generators malfunctioned, and a caregiver model tried to intervene and short circuited. Fortunately, no human patients had died as a result, but the caregiver model Rosy, a brave G-4, sacrificed her life.

Betty tried calling Tom and Meg, but realized they would still be on the plane during this time. She hadn't told anyone else about the babies. She felt it only proper that aside from the Kerrings, Mack should be the first to know.

Betty knew she had to calm down. Much like a human's heartbeat and adrenaline, the more her processors sped up, the more power it would take for her to operate. The bulk of her power had to go to maintaining the children, their filtration, and nutrient release. She started thinking about her situation.

Now I see the wisdom the Kerrings had in not having the G-3s be mobile. I thought it was cruel, but they were right.

Betty self-comforted, sitting down holding her tummy, and rocking herself back and forth wondering what to do. She tried the Kerrings several times in her mind. Dr. Kerring's voicemail box was full. She finally left a message on Robert's voicemail:

"Robbie?" Betty was whimpering. *"Everything went*

terribly wrong when I tried to tell Mack. He basically ran out of the house and left to I don't know where. I went over closer to him but he backed away every single time, and then he left me Robbie! He said he needed time to think, and he left me! What am I going to do? The poor babies!"

She kept whimpering uncontrollably until she realized the voicemail box had run out of time and hung up on her.

Betty felt even more vulnerable and alone than that first time when Jimmy had pushed her onto the floor of the maintenance closet and handcuffed her to the shelves. She literally had nowhere to turn to. She decided to sleep and charge, thinking it might make her feel better. Afterward, she tried calling Mack. He did not pick up, so she left a message:

"Mack, I know you're upset with me. Please don't be. I only wanted to give you as precious of a gift as you gave to me. I wanted so badly to be a mother to your and Miri's children. I love them Mack, they are a part of me too! A boy and a girl. It was cruel that they should be frozen in time. They deserve to live, and to be happy with parents who love them and who love each other. I wanted to surprise you with them when I knew they had reached the stage where they were healthy and well. I wanted to make you a father. Please don't be mad at me Mack. I love you so much!"

Then, she got hung up on. She tried again, but the voice mailbox was full.

Chapter 9
Just a Walk in the Park

Betty decided to sleep again and intentionally charged extra, having plenty of power in her reserve battery backup.

To take her mind off things just a bit, she thought she would go out for a walk by herself. It would be nice to go to the nearby park to just sit and watch kids playing and hear the birds singing. She dearly loved being around nature.

Betty got to the park a bit after 3 p.m. It was starting to cheer her up. She stopped to examine some pretty flowers and watched some insects as they busied themselves with their tasks. Some people looked at her a bit strangely when she sat on the ground to get a closer look at some pigeons. She mimicked their coos with exact precision, and they came running over to her, bobbing their little heads as they walked. One even got up on her outstretched finger.

"I'm sorry little ones, I don't have any food for you."

As if they understood her, they flew off. She started talking to the babies using her internal speaker. She likely had a closer relationship with them than most human mothers could ever achieve, because her internal speaker could allow them to hear her voice softly speaking to them, and she could also see them in her mind with her ultrasound scanning equipment as they developed.

Giovanni Marino was an old-fashioned gangster, whose preferred method of killing people was to dump their bodies tied up and weighted down into the nearest body of water available. His family was from a long line of sailors and pirates, and once they got into organized crime, it seemed only natural that they gravitated to water.

Gio was paranoid about the government watching him and had the GPS systems disconnected from almost all his newer cars. He refused to use cellphones because they could be tracked or listened in on, and he had others do all his dirty work, which enabled him to literally get away with murder.

Melissa was one of Gio's newest con artists. She had charmed and convinced James Simmons of a way to take money from Quality First, which, unknown to him would ultimately go to Gio and his organization. She learned of Mack's address after Jimmy had hired a private detective to find out where Betty was hiding before her freedom trial took place. Melissa dutifully reported it all to Gio.

Now, Gio had not forgotten about Betty or her "debt" to him, from her helping the authorities retrieve the money that Melissa and Jimmy took from Quality First. After Melissa's botched kidnapping of Meg, and the idea she told him, Gio sent two of his goons around to case the area where Betty and Mack lived. Mack's apartment was very private and secure, and the doorman helped a lot to discourage trespassers.

About a month had gone by, and the guys were nearly ready to give up. They had been waiting and watching in their parked van for the moment when they might see Betty go out alone on foot. Today was finally their chance! As they saw her leave, they got out of their van, went to the side door and got a black hood and handcuffs. They stuck them in a satchel along with some sandwiches, since they always seemed to be hungry.

They followed her to the park, again watching and waiting for an opportune time when no one else would be around.

"What's with this crazy chick? She acts like a little kid!" remarked Alfred, a taller, thin man of about forty-five.

"I don't know, but the Boss said to bring her back alive. She must be pretty important," replied his shorter friend Leo, a fortyish, balding man with a thick New York accent.

"She should be easy to get. I mean look at her. She's sitting on the ground talking to the birds!" He chuckled.

"I don't think we can just 'Bag, Bind 'n' Bring,'" Alfred said.

They approached Betty, appearing to be concerned citizens.

"Good afternoon. Did you lose something down there?" Leo bent over and smiled, his hands behind his back.

Betty got up, realizing she must have looked kind of odd.

"No Sir. I was watching some pigeons, but they flew off. I just continued to sit where I was." She smiled back. "I was just about to leave. I should be getting back home." Betty read their micro-expressions. They seemed dishonest.

"There can be some real creeps in the park sometimes," Alfred said. "We can walk with you on your way home."

Something does not seem quite right with these men, she thought to herself. *They seem far too intent on hanging around me. How can I possibly lose them or make them go?*

Leo said, "Yeah, a pretty young lady like yourself? It could be dangerous walking around here all alone."

Against her better judgement, she let them walk along with her, hoping they would eventually just leave her alone.

"I'm Leo, and this big guy here is Alfred. We'll take care of you." Leo offered to shake her hand.

"We're all friends here, what's your name?" Alfred asked.

"Betty is my name," she said warily, not wanting to say her last name. Mack had warned her that robot haters might still remember her from the trial.

The guys looked at each other and nodded, this was the right lady. They kept walking with her and arrived at the van.

"This is our stop," Leo said as he opened his satchel. He reached in to get something. Betty assumed it was keys to his van.

"Well, it was nice meeting you, and thanks for walking me most of the way home," Betty replied, facing Leo. She tried to be polite and started to go, but Leo stepped directly in front of her.

Alfred went around behind her, sliding the van's side door open and said sternly, "Maybe you don't understand, Betty. Leo said, this is our stop. That means, all of us!"

Betty turned around to look at Alfred, and Leo jerked the black hood over her head from behind. Alfred quickly cuffed her; they pushed her into the van and slid the door shut. They both ran to the front of the van, got in and sped off.

"See, a piece of cake!" Alfred grinned at Leo.

Betty felt she was moving and realized what had happened. She had no idea where they were going. It was a very old van and had no GPS or any kind of onboard computer. She tried to locate some sort of mobile devices, but these guys had nothing.

She called the Kerrings, but with their major emergency, no one was available. She tried Tom and Meg, but still there was no answer. She tried Mack but his voicemail box was full.

Well, if I can't talk to a human to try to come and find me, maybe I can at least leave text messages, she thought. *I wanted freedom, and this is the cost of not being monitored.*

She tried to leave texts for someone to help her, and that she had been kidnapped; that they would have to locate her by her GPS signal. She kept a level head, snapping out of her sad mood. Instead of crying about her condition, she thought of her babies. She was programmed not to defend herself, but having two human lives inside her to protect was a whole different story.

Unfortunately, it seemed everyone was busy, and didn't even think to check their phones for any kind of messages.

Leo and Alfred arrived at an old warehouse. They carried Betty into the antiquated building made of one-foot-thick walls of solid brick, with a stone foundation. There was an old rickety freight elevator that they took down to the dark, damp basement. It jerked to a stop, and they opened the old scissor gate doors, brought Betty out and dumped her on the floor. She curled up as she felt herself falling so the ectogenesis pod would stay protected. They dragged her into to a room, closed and locked the squeaky old door. She heard them start the elevator again.

She managed to wriggle the hood off her head, then used her infrared sight to view her surroundings. There was nothing really warm or alive there, but thermal energy was reflected off of some of the objects in the relatively empty room: an old utility tub with a leaky faucet, and a folded chair propped against the wall.

Another one of those hard, steel folding chairs, and handcuffs. Really? Betty shuddered. She then switched to her ultraviolet spectrum of vision, and what showed up for her was horrifying! There were many organic substances splattered on walls, smeared on the chair, but mostly it was on the floor leading to a drain. Some glowed a bright yellow green, but the majority showed up as black, which meant it was most likely blood. There was an array of tools hanging on the wall from a pegboard: a hacksaw, wire cutters, needle nose pliers and a big bolt cutter. They all had the black residue.

Where am I? What is this place? But more importantly, how long am I to be staying here? I must conserve my energy for the children. She went into sleep mode, with a minimal amount of her various sensing capabilities enabled.

Alfred and Leo drove to Scarolie's, Gio's favorite hangout. They knew he usually ate there around this time. It was now about 5 p.m. They came into the restaurant and plopped themselves down at his table, grinning.

"We got her Boss!" Leo went to pick up one of Gio's breadsticks, but he grabbed Leo's hand before he got to it.

"Hey! Didn't your mother teach you any manners?" Gio shoved Leo's hand away.

Alfred at least greeted him properly. "Hi Gio. We have her down at the warehouse in the special room. She came pretty quietly. All our recon work paid off. Come on over and you can see her for yourself."

"Alright gentlemen. Let me finish my dinner, and we'll all go over and see this famous Betty together."

Gio finished all his food, took the napkin off his lap, patted his mouth with the corner, and placed it on the table.

"Check please!" he yelled over the restaurant noise. Gio left in his sports car, and his goons followed in their old van.

Betty heard them coming in the elevator. They unlocked the old squeaky door, jerked it open and turned on a light switch.

"Here she is!" Leo and Alfred said at the same time.

"Perché non si muove?" Gio asked. "Ti avevo detto di riportarla in vita! She's a hero, but worth nothing dead!"

They didn't know that Betty could really understand them.

She analyzed it in her mind: *"Perché non si muove? Ti avevo detto di riportarla in vita!"* Italian; Translation: *"Why isn't she moving? I told you to bring her alive!"*

"Well, Boss," Leo fumbled for words, "she was alive when we left her. And look at that, she managed to get the hood off." The three men walked around her and nudged her with their feet. Nothing happened, she just stayed still, although she was totally aware of their presence.

"Come on guys, let's get her up on this chair," Gio said.

Leo was determined to prove she wasn't dead and that they succeeded in their mission, so they could get paid. They grabbed her and set her on the chair in a sitting position. Still conserving as much energy as she could, she only opened her eyes.

"Alright! You are alive. So, this is the famous Betty Fourré!" Gio announced. "Uh, Betty Fourré Schwartz, that is. My friend Melissa has told me so much about you! Good to finally meet you. So. You're really not human, huh?"

Gio walked around the chair trying to intimidate her and did a very good job at it too. She only followed him with her eyes the whole time, not making even a single expression.

"If I didn't know any better, I would never be able to tell." He squatted down in front of her and looked her in the eyes.

"Whaddya mean she's not human?" a puzzled Leo asked.

"That's right guys. Betty here is a robot, and she's responsible for taking all my money away, isn't that right

Betty?" Gio yelled at her. "So, tell me Betty. How do you work? How are you going to get me my money back?" She still sat quietly. "I want answers, and I want them now!"

He dumped her off the chair, and again she rolled into a fetal position to protect the children. She closed her eyes.

"This ain't working Boss, she ain't talking! I don't think you're gonna get her to do what you want, without a little friendly persuasion." Leo grinned, rubbing his hands together.

"Leo, just how do you propose I persuade her?"

"Gee, I dunno Boss. Maybe slap her around a bit?"

"And that would accomplish what? Maybe damage her computer brain so she can't hack into the bank and get my money back?" Gio smacked Leo on the side of his head.

"Sorry Boss." Leo finally shut up, slightly cowering.

"What about waterboarding her?" Alfred asked Gio.

"Are you guys total idiots?" Gio retorted. "She would probably short-circuit before we'd get anything out of her. What do you think, she's waterproof? She's a robot!"

Little did they know that she really was waterproof, as long as her mouth was closed, and her diagnostic port's gasket was firmly in place. Even her "belly buttons" were sealed tightly with the connectors firmly screwed into place to drain the filtration system and refill the nutrient tank fluid.

Betty's mouth was so incredibly strong that she probably could easily bite their fingers off if they got in the way of her closing it. Once clamped down automatically when moisture was present, no water could get in. Robert had built-in safety features, so that caregivers could bathe patients or be submerged in order to rescue someone if they slipped under the water.

"Alright, if she's not going to talk, I suggest we ask for ransom money for her. She's basically a national treasure."

Gio saw the red, white, and blue ribbon of her medal of honor sticking out of her collar. She was so proud of it that she wore it around her neck under her clothes and rarely took it off.

"Look at this, guys!" He took off her medal. "You don't see these every day. We'll send this with a ransom note for seventy mil. I was going to take off a finger, but this is even better. Now we just need to figure out where to send it."

"You think the lawyer's got seventy mil?" Leo had a point.

"Well, where should we send it then, the White House?" Geo said sarcastically. "You want the Secret Service involved too?"

Betty knew she had to say something. "Caring Corp. Contact Dr. Kenneth Kerring of Caring Corp. He will pay you that kind of money for me. The address is 20677 Caring Way," she said groggily, and went back into sleep mode.

"She speaks! Now do as she says, and prepare the ransom note," Gio ordered them. They turned out the light and left.

Alfred and Leo got together the contents for the package, typed out a ransom note, and sealed it all up, ready to send express mail, barely getting it there in time to overnight.

Chapter 10
Robot for Ransom

Mack had just been sitting at a bus stop bench for several hours, seriously contemplating all that transpired between him and Betty. Once he stopped being in shock after having a chance to clear his head, he suddenly had an epiphany as he thought.

What is the matter with me? Betty is the sweetest person in the world. She would never do anything to intentionally hurt me. How could I have so callously disregarded the wonderful news she gave me? They're my own children! I am so embarrassed by how I reacted. How could I have ever treated her like that!

He got very upset at himself the more he thought about it.

She's very right, of what use is it for them to just sit there frozen indefinitely? She found out about them and tried to give me the most priceless gift, it's true! How could I run out on her like that? How must she be feeling? So much for "honoring your wife more than yourself" like a proper Jewish husband. I need to swallow my pride and go back to her right now. I owe her an apology, and need to tell her how special and loved she really is!

Mack reached into his pocket to grab his phone, but being so tired the evening before, he had forgotten to turn it back on after he got off the plane. He saw Betty had called him once and played back her very special message. It made him feel even worse about how he reacted. He had to go to her immediately!

What a fool I have been, so wrapped up in mourning over the past that I couldn't see the potential for the future staring me right in the face! he thought, feeling ashamed.

He tried to get back to their apartment as fast as he could. On the way home, he bought some flowers, knowing how much Betty loved them. She was fascinated by their natural beauty. She liked to alternate her vision to view them in visible light as a human would see in, then switch to the ultraviolet spectrum to look at them in all their glowing, psychedelic colors.

Betty was trying in vain to call everyone; anyone, text or email, use her GPS to find her location, and even tried sending a distress signal with her new transmitter, but being below ground within the confines of a solid rock foundation in the huge old building, nothing got through. Gio loved this building for that very reason. Having been built back in the mid-1800s, it was essentially like a fortress. It helped ease his paranoia of getting caught by the Feds. Several shell companies were used to mask its ownership, but it had been in his family since the days of prohibition. It was huge, having myriads of tunnels and concealed back entrances. Just as in the days of bootlegging, it was an ideal place to set up shop undetected, for his drug manufacturing operations.

All Betty could do now, was conserve her power as long as she could, so she stopped even trying to reach anyone. Not planning to be at the park for very long and since it was relatively close by, she hadn't brought her charger with her. If her main power went down too low, at least she had a little reserve backup battery. By now, it was nearly sunset, around 8 p.m. on August fourth. She had a full charge and reserve that afternoon before she left, but when would she be released?

Stay calm, she thought to herself. *Just keep going into sleep mode to conserve power and keep those babies alive!*

Mack arrived home. He set his things down and went to the kitchen to put the flowers in a pretty vase to surprise Betty. She still hadn't come to him as she normally did. Since his voicemail box had been full, she was unable to leave him another message saying that she had been taken. He had no idea.

Merely thinking that she was likely upset at him and rightfully so, he thought perhaps she was hiding from him. He called out to her, "Please come out Betty. I love you! I'm so, so sorry. It was very wrong of me to leave! Everything is fine now, you'll see. I'll be a perfect husband and father from now on." But she was nowhere to be found in his apartment.

Robert called up Mack very upset. "We just got done with an emergency at Caring Corp. and I played all of Betty's messages. What did you say to her? She was crying!"

Dr. Kerring heard what Robert said to Mack and immediately asked, "What has he done to my girl?" He had never gotten any messages from her because his voicemail box had been full during their emergency. Robert motioned to his father to calm down, and he would explain later.

Robert continued, "You know how sensitive she is. Mack, I thought you loved her and would take care of her!"

"I do love her, and yes, I know. I feel so terrible about it. I just got home. I came back to apologize and make things right, but I can't find Betty anywhere!" Mack was getting very concerned. "Robert, what is going on?"

"Betty's been kidnapped! It sounded like, she said she was in a car or something. But then she stopped calling, and I can't locate her GPS or her transmitter. I almost think she might be dead!" Robert choked back some tears.

"Someone took her?" Mack confirmed. "I warned her about the robot haters. But how did they get to her? This is all my fault, I should have never left, but I'm only human. I needed some time to think. I was just, kind of in shock."

"That is water under the bridge, Mack. Please don't dwell on it. Now, let's all put our heads together and figure out what to do. Have you gotten any kind of ransom note?" Robert asked.

"Nothing was left here at my door while I was out."

Robert instructed Mack, "Maybe you should stay there and wait in case anyone contacts you or you hear something. Let's all stay in touch until we know how to proceed."

It was a night of intense waiting for the Kerrings and Mack. Betty stayed in sleep mode much of the time, and Gio and his goons all went home. Nothing could really be done until the ransom note was received the next morning.

The next day, an express mail truck finally arrived, delivering a small package addressed to Caring Corp. "From Betty" was the recipient name, and there was no return address; nothing handwritten. Robert unwrapped the brown paper, then slowly opened the lid on the box. Inside were layers of tissue paper. He took off the first layer, and there was Betty's medal of honor. He phoned Mack and had his father come to the office, telling them what he received.

"It's a plain paper and looks typed. I'll read it. It says, 'On August fifth at midnight . . .'"

"Wait, that's tonight!" Robert continued reading aloud . . .

"'Put seventy million dollars in unmarked bills in a duffel bag and bring it to Washington Park. Just northwest of the Johnson Memorial is the Knox Street Mall. Keep going along the path until you reach a bench that has an arrow spray painted on the ground next to it. It points to a nearby recycle can. Put the duffel bag in that can and leave it there. Once we have the money, we will set Betty free in an undetermined location and she will get in contact with you to pick her up. Do not involve the cops. One person comes alone to drop it off. Involve the cops, she's dead. Less than seventy million, she's dead. We mean business.'"

"Okay, that sounds simple enough," Robert said. "I'm not sure how we'll come up with the money, but we have to."

Robert worked on getting the money together. His father volunteered to be the one to go there, so that Robert could keep checking on trying to track Betty's transmitter or GPS.

"All set Dad?" Robert asked. His father gave a thumbs up. "I still have no signal yet." Mack came over to Caring Corp. to be with the Kerrings. Nobody could sleep anyway.

It was about 11:45 p.m. and Dr. Kerring made his way to Washington Park. He got to the memorial, walked a bit, and saw the arrow. He was about to put the bag into the can when a pair of police officers on foot patrol came over to him. There had been drug deals going on in the area, so they suspected anyone that looked like they had drugs or money.

"Good evening, Sir. What may I ask, brings you to the park at this hour of the night?" one officer said suspiciously.

Dr. Kerring didn't know how to respond. He wasn't expecting any policemen to be there, the kidnappers specifically said not to involve any cops!

"I'm, just taking a stroll. It's nice and cool right now. My favorite time of night, ha-ha-ha." He laughed awkwardly.

"What do you have in the bag Sir?" the other officer asked and came over shining his flashlight on it.

"Oh, nothing really important Officers, I was just going to recycle this bag." Dr. Kerring went and started to go over to put the duffel bag in the recycling can.

The second officer shook his head no. "Stop what you

are doing right now. I will ask again Sir. What is in the bag? It doesn't look like recyclable material to me."

"I have to throw it out. Please officers, I have to throw it out!" Dr. Kerring was just about in tears.

"Show us what's in the bag Sir. I am not going to ask you again." Dr. Kerring tried to take it over to the recycle can, but they stood in the way insisting to see what was in it.

"Very interesting Sir. That's a whole of a lot of money you are uh, just throwing out. Alright. You're coming with us and bringing the bag. We don't take drug deals lightly, and there have been far too many going down in this area."

"But officers, I'm not here to buy drugs." Then he raised his voice in a panic, "I'm Doctor Kerring with Caring Corp."

"Doctor, right! You must have sold drugs then. Save it for your lawyer. Let's go." They escorted him away with the bag.

Alfred had been watching from a distance, concealed by trees and scrubby bushes. He went to the van and drove back to the warehouse, where Gio was waiting to get his money.

"Well? How'd it go Alfie?" He rubbed his hands together vigorously in anticipation. "I can't wait to see all that cash!"

"There was a problem, Gio." Alfred looked worried.

"You know I don't like problems Alfred." Gio started getting upset. "Didn't anyone show?"

"Well yeah, he showed at midnight. I was there and I saw everything. I heard him clearly say he was Dr. Kerring of the

Caring Corp. so that was definitely our guy. Unfortunately, he met two cops there, and it looked like they convinced him not to do the deal after all. Then they all left with the bag.”

“What? I told them no cops! They reneged on the deal?”

“What are we gonna do with the robot Boss? She can recognize us all now!” Leo looked irritated.

Gio looked at Betty, “I don’t know if you are still conscious or not, but you could have helped yourself by getting us the money back when you had the chance. That’s all it would have taken! Such a waste.” Gio shook his head.

“You’re right Leo. If she did survive, she could recognize and identify us. Bring her upstairs to the main floor.”

Gio motioned to Leo and Alfred, “Okay guys, you know what to do. Go get concrete blocks and some chain. Hop to it!”

Leo laughed. “Looks like you’re gonna go for a swim!”

Betty was still in sleep mode, so to the rest of the world, she looked dead. She only had the limited amount of sound detection on, so that she could be aware of what was happening. She knew that they were moving her, so she thought she might need some clues as to her location. She briefly opened her eyes and filmed everything. They brought her up the creaky service elevator and traipsed through the warehouse where their main drug operation was going on.

Once they reached the front office, she stopped recording, quickly sent it to the cloud, closed her eyes, and went into sleep mode. They dumped her on the floor of the office. She curled up as usual, and they left the room to go get their supplies.

Leo and Alfred came to Betty and dropped some chain down and set a couple of concrete blocks next to her.

"Let's get her up so we can wrap the chain around her middle," Leo instructed Alfred. "I think she's already dead, but you know the Boss, he likes to make sure."

They carried her over to a grimy looking couch that was in the office room and put her on it. They started to wrap the chain around her, but as soon as Alfred reached her abdominal area where her babies could be endangered, she instinctively used her powerful legs to keep him away and kicked him across the room.

"Uffff!" Alfred huffed as he thudded against the wall.

"Heh-heh-heh!" Leo laughed at Alfred's outcome. "Well, I guess she ain't dead after all, Alfie! Heh-heh-heh."

Leo still managed to get the chain wrapped all around her, but she manipulated it away from the lower part of her tummy at least. Leo noticed that so long as the chain wasn't around her lower abdomen, she didn't fight him at all.

Leo chuckled. "So, you wanna be comfortable, do you? That's okay. I told you we'd take care of you." She stayed still, holding her belly to protect it. Alfred warily got up but stayed clear of her legs. They would later attach each end of the chain to a concrete block when they got to the river.

"I'll go tell the Boss that she's ready to go, you can go

get the van." Alfred nodded, still smarting from Betty's kick.

Alfred went to get the van, and brought it around to the front, then went inside. Leo had informed Gio that they were taking Betty's body to dump in the Hudson River, as was Gio's tradition. She stayed still the whole time, holding her arms around her belly and her eyes were closed. She went stiff and rigid, all joints locked into place, and jaws clamped shut.

Since she was out of the basement, Betty tried texting Robert in her mind since it took less power than phoning:

"Robbie plz txt back if U get this."

"Oh good! It's Betty," he said to Mack and texted back: `"Betty, are you OK? We're worried sick about you! Can we come get you?"`

"Follow GPS & transmitter. On land now. Am 2 B dumped N H2O soon. GPS not trackable N H20. Must save power. No charge N 2 days. Been N sleep mode 2 conserve NRG. BBs OK 4 now but power LO! Must protect @ ALL costs." `"OK Betty, we will track you and try to find you."` Robert texted her back as fast as he could.

Alfred commented, "She must be dead now. Look, she's stiff. The rigor mortis has already set in!"

"The Boss said she's a robot Alfie. She wouldn't have that," Leo responded. "She probably just ran out of power. I can almost guarantee you she'll rust away in the water."

Chapter 11
Betty's Legacy

Dr. Kerring was brought into the police station, where he tried to convince them that he had to drop the money off in the park, not collect it. They almost arrested him, but there was insufficient evidence of his trying to buy or sell drugs.

Finally, he could not hold back any longer and started crying that some people had kidnapped his daughter, he was only following instructions and wasn't allowed to involve the police. He had them contact his lawyer Maccabee Schwartz, who corroborated the story.

Betty's alarms were sounding in her head that she was low on her main power. She turned them off and was now running solely on her reserve backup battery. She made sure her transmitter beacon and GPS were activated but could do nothing more than go into sleep mode for as long as she could. She begrudgingly shut down the filtration system and nutrient timer, since the babies were still tiny enough that they could possibly get by without them for a short period of time. She set her timer for two hours. When that timer went off, she would have to use one last burst of energy to do a final filtration round and a nutrient shot, using every little bit of power she had left. After that, it would be over for the three of them.

After driving about a half an hour, Gio's goons arrived at a private spot by the river near some railroad tracks.

"This is the good spot, right Leo?" Leo nodded and Alfred stopped the van. They got out and carried Betty over to the riverbank, then brought over the concrete blocks, setting them next to her. They secured each end of the chain to a block, fastening them in place with clips, then brought over an inflated pool raft, put her on it and placed the blocks on her legs. Slipping into their boot-footed waders, Leo and Alfred got in the water guiding Betty out as far as they could go and overturned the raft, then down she sank into the water. Arriving back at the shore with the raft, they took off their waders, threw everything into the van, got in and sped off.

Underwater, Betty was in sleep mode, but for some reason, she felt like she was totally conscious. She saw visions in her mind like in dreams. As it faded in, she saw the world as if she were a child. Playing with a teddy bear, tag with friends, high school, then she saw Mack. He looked so young! There was a wedding; the now notable event of Mack unsuccessfully trying to break the glass, until finally it gave way, then the crowd shouted "Mazal Tov." *Am I remembering Ma's picture album?* she thought.

Later, she saw a car accident, flinging herself over Mack's body to protect him, a hospital room and then everything went completely white. But these weren't her memories. Was she delirious? Was she hallucinating? Short-circuiting in the water had always been her worst possible fear.

She then thought back to when she herself had just been created, back at Caring Corp. and the times of being in the "Preschool" room, where she was comprehending how her body interacted with her computer mind's programming. She was sitting on the floor, shaking her arms up and down as a baby would do, learning gradually how to maneuver them; her processors speeding and her AI was in intense learning mode.

Once their bodies were fully tuned to their mind, models went to what they affectionately called the "School", where they had human teachers to help guide and monitor the progress of these new caregivers-to-be. AI-based computers could be programmed to some extent, but the Caring Corp. models were taught interactions with humans, by humans.

Then she remembered the "Social Studies" class, where the models learned to match and harmonize facial expressions with natural speech and develop instinctive reactions. She saw all the various sections at Caring Corp.

Betty recalled when she helped create the logo for Caring Corp. It had to express "care", with the two Cs intertwined. She had asked Dr. Kerring about the history of the company name, so he told her the story of how he chose it. Being a humble man, he didn't really want the company to be named after himself. Back then, his wife Cara suggested changing the spelling slightly. He thought it was a great idea and insisted it should be a combination of their names, "Car" for Cara, "ring" for Kerring, and of course "Caring" was a homonym for "Kerring", indicative of the services they provided for people. It was truly a family business. Their daughter April was born after that, and Robert came along five years later.

Now, instead of just remembering past times, in her head she again saw visions; vivid scenes of her own life after her code tweaking. She was enjoying all these "movies" in her head and they weren't seeming to be using any extra power.

Then she saw Leela, dear Leela! She was up and about, looking healthier. Then the vision fast forwarded to her sad end. Leela was commenting that her life was being played in front of her, just like a movie. She said that she was reliving everything she had experienced in life in just a few brief minutes, right before she died there in Betty's arms.

Is that what this is? Betty thought. *Am I dying, and this is my life flashing before my eyes? My babies, I don't want to lose my babies; Mack and Miri's sweet babies. Would they have been better off to have just remained frozen? Have I killed them too? What have I done?*

Her "dreams" continued. Jimmy brought her to Quality First. She met Meg, then Mack, saved people on the plane, stopped the hijackers. She attended Meg and Tom's wedding, caught the bouquet. She married Mack with Tom and Meg by their sides. The court case, where she won her freedom, her decision to give Mack the gift of fatherhood. Now, she had reached the end. She heard a voice saying, "Tell the rabbi everything. Talk to all three, they will know what to do."

Her backup battery alarm had been going off for several minutes. Her transmitter stopped. She had no more power. Finally, every function inside of Betty completely ceased.

Once Dr. Kerring had the police get in touch with Mack to prove that there had indeed been a kidnapping, they sent a team out into the field. They were corresponding with Robert, as he was tracking Betty's GPS while she was still on land, but then it stopped and disappeared as she went underwater. He tried her emergency transmitter beacon and pinpointed the location where the signal last showed up. He went out to meet them in the Caring Corp. van, with the coordinates of that last known location where Betty had transmitted from.

The current of the river was not very strong tonight, but it still could potentially carry her body away from the exact spot, making it difficult to locate her. There were now helicopters and patrol cars starting to swarm around the area of the riverbank. Divers with high-powered flashlights went into the water looking for Betty.

At 2 a.m., one of the divers located her, and they found another body too, as it turned out. The other person, or what remained of them, had also been chained to concrete blocks.

It would take a long time to identify what was left of the other body. Due to the sensitive nature and to protect Betty, nothing was released to the press yet about the discovery and recovery of the people they found that night.

They brought Betty out. Her skin was starting to get a bit puffy, but it was all intact. Her arms were still clutching on to her tummy. The police unwrapped the chains and got her free. Robert came running over. She was now very cold, and it had been one hour since she her timer went off to alert her that her reserve power was out of time. She had given the babies all the power that she could to provide one last session of filtration and a final nutrient release, before the reserve backup battery was exhausted and all her functions totally stopped.

"Betty, Betty, Sis!" Robert yelled, but there was no response. He had brought along a charger, but of course, there was no place to plug in there at the river.

"We are doctors, and she needs to get to Caring Corp. immediately! Can any of you escort us there? This is Betty Fourré Schwartz, the national hero! She is our relative." The Kerrings loaded Betty into their Caring Corp. van.

"Sure, I remember Betty. She had her picture taken with a bunch of us after her court case. We can escort you there, just lead the way," one of the officers said. He got into a car with his partner, and they started up the siren and lights. They would follow closely behind.

Dr. Kenneth Kerring got in the driver's seat and Robert took care of Betty in the back. The van was well-equipped with plenty of chargers, power cords, and auxiliary ports for charging, just as the models used in their direct charging beds. Robert patted the area on the back of Betty's neck dry with one of the many towels he had brought, removed the gasket and plugged in her diagnostic port to charge her.

"Dad, I don't like how cold she is. I have never felt her cold before. I'm scared for her. How long can the semi-organic skin remain unheated?" Robert patted her dry all over. She was still rigid, but her skin was getting less puffy. Caregivers were not usually in the water for longer than a half hour at most, tending to patients or showering. It seemed that her cultured-skin cells were absorbing water over a longer period of time. Fortunately, it did not seep into the internal parts of her body.

"I think it will be okay Robert. Keep in mind, for cryopreservation of cells, they need to be cold. It would be more detrimental if she had overheated. Now, I'm not saying this is good for her, but it might not be bad." Dr. Kerring kept driving, and the police car behind them kept the siren on.

"I can't tell if she's charging. The monitor shows no activity at all." Robert was afraid for her. "We should never have done her procedure, we probably endangered her life, and the fetuses."

Finally, his monitor showed a blip of something. It was slow to show but he could see a trickle charge going into her.

"She's getting something Dad, but it just isn't enough. It has been so long that I fear the fetuses won't make it. At this point I don't know if Betty will even make it. Where is Mack?"

Dr. Kerring answered, "I told him to go to his apartment and try to get some sleep. He would probably just get in the way and is likely far too upset to deal with the scene. I even have a hard time seeing her like this."

"But shouldn't we call him? At least to say that we found her?" Robert continued drying her off as best he could.

"I'm still upset at him for treating Betty the way he did. Let him sit there and get a taste of his own medicine wondering what happened to her. We don't know how she is yet anyway. We need to get her home to a proper lab and charging bed." Indeed, Dr. Kerring was "very protective of the women in his life" as Robert had once said to Betty.

They arrived at Caring Corp. and got out of the van. Dr. Kerring thanked the police officers profusely for their help.

One of the caregiver models inside brought out a stretcher. They got Betty on it and wheeled her inside to Robert's diagnostics lab room. They all brought her over to the charging bed and hooked her up to a monitor to determine her status and have her charge faster. Finally, there was a little more activity.

"She's charging Dad! I'm not seeing any programming functions going on, but it shows her battery is finally taking slightly more than a trickle charge." Robert had a little bit of hope.

Chapter 12
Recovery

"What does it all mean Robert, will Betty be okay? And what about the babies? Maybe we should hook them up to an external system. Also, if Betty's monitor isn't working on the inside, we should do an abdominal ultrasound from the outside, just as pregnant humans would usually get. We need to ascertain how those babies are doing. Or if they're even doing."

Dr. Kerring went to get a G-3 model stand that had the filtration unit and nutrient tank in the bottom already in place.

"You aren't going to remove her legs, are you Dad?" Robert frowned looking at his father. "She would never forgive you!"

"No, nothing like that Robert. My interest right now is in getting the babies what they need, if they're still okay."

Dr. Kerring brought over a portable ultrasound machine and was viewing the little ones on the screen. He zoomed in on them and saw that they were actually moving. They were just far enough along at ten weeks, that movement could be detected.

"Look Robert, we have signs of life!" He joyously showed his son the babies. "I've got to get that filtration system and the nutrient flow going to them."

He hooked up the devices in the G-3 stand to Betty so they could take over the filtration and nutrient supply until she was restored to working order, if she could be. At this point, Betty's computer mind appeared to be the equivalent of brain-dead.

Robert kept checking the monitors, "Still showing a bit more than a trickle charge. Come on Betty, please wake up. Get charging! Your babies need you. Betty come back!"

That little bit of information seemed to be enough to jolt her into a faster charging mode.

"I think maybe it was only charging her reserve battery at first, and then now it is going to the main. Betty, you scared me!" She still was not responding. It concerned him greatly.

Did the water somehow get to her? Did a total depletion of all her battery power do major damage? Robert pondered.

At least now she was getting more than just a trickle charge. However, it could potentially take a few hours for her to charge to relatively normal power levels. Only time would tell.

As Dr. Kerring hooked up the tubing to Betty for the nutrient release and filtration systems, Robert watched Betty's diagnostics closely. The babies were doing well. However, she herself wasn't so fortunate. It was 4 a.m. and she still had no noticeable activity in her computer brain. It only showed that she was at least holding a charge in her main battery.

Dr. Kerring was satisfied that the babies were okay for now, but he had to go home and sleep. If for some reason Betty wouldn't make it, they could transfer the ectogenesis pod to a G-3 to carry to full term. Robert stayed there by Betty's side.

Mack was still at his apartment waiting. He had no idea

what was going on. *Where is Betty? Did they find her? Is she okay? Are the babies okay?* Mack wondered to himself. He certainly got his payback for treating Betty so harshly and prayed that she and the babies would survive and be alright.

Mack wasn't able to sleep all night. Just as the sun barely started peeking over the horizon, he finally dozed off and started dreaming. Instead of his usual nightmares he had of the accident, he was sitting there peacefully with Miri on the couch. She stroked his hair and said, "Don't worry Mack, I am right here with you. Everything will be fine. I will always love you and be here for you in any way that I can. Our children will grow up to be strong and healthy. Just you wait and see!"

Then he woke up with a start. His dream had seemed so real! It was alarming yet comforting. But it was also a bit strange. He and Miri never had living children together before. And how could Miri be there for him if she was gone?

Robert was still there after the sun came up, watching Betty and waiting. It was now 7 a.m. and the lab workers would be coming to work in about an hour. He was about to give up, when finally, after over five hours of constant charging, the monitor beeped and showed some computer brain activity!

"Betty, are you there?" Robert asked. She still wasn't verbally responding, but the monitor seemed to indicate that there were some functions starting up. Her heating elements had activated, so she started getting warmer. It helped to dry out her skin so that it was no longer puffy or wrinkled, then her jaws finally unlocked. One by one, other functions started up.

An alarm on his computer started beeping, indicating that her filtration and nutrient tanks were not connected or functioning. That was a good sign that proved her tank monitors were working. Now his computer was showing she had processor activity! Her simulated heartbeat and breathing patterns that matched her processor speed started sounding, and Betty opened her eyes. She blinked a few times, moved her head slowly back and forth, then looked over at Robert who was there next to her.

"Hey Sis, are you okay?" he asked her, speaking softly.

"Robbie!" Betty whispered, slowly smiling at him. "I'm so stiff." She closed her eyes, and exercised her stiffened linkage joints, taking an inventory check of all moving parts; however, one thing concerned her even more. "How are the babies?"

"The babies will be fine Betty. I have no idea how you managed it, but you kept them alive, and they are doing well. You always amaze me, Sis." He beamed at her in admiration.

"You had me so scared! No model has ever drained their power completely that I am aware of. And to be carrying fetuses too? That's simply unheard of!"

She suddenly looked around, then up at Robert with a terrified expression and started whimpering. "Where's Mack? Is he still mad at me? I don't want to live without him!"

"He's okay, he came back to you on his own. We haven't

told him anything yet, because frankly, I wasn't sure if you were even going to make it! I'll call him right now, he's worried sick about you. Please rest some more and charge Betty. You're not fully functional yet. And . . ." Robert went to get something.

"I believe this belongs to you?" He hung her gold medal up within her sight. He then placed her hands on her belly.

"Feel that? The babies are still in there, although Dad had to connect the ectogenesis pod to an external system temporarily, just until we knew that you would be functioning properly." She smiled then went into sleep and maintenance mode and continued charging as Robert had instructed her.

Robert went to call, as promised. "Hello Mack? I have news for you. Betty was found in the Hudson River by the divers, and they brought her up. We rushed her back to Caring Corp."

"How is she? Is she okay? I just could not be able to take losing my wife a second time. How are the babies?"

"The babies are stable and doing fine, but Betty was not even responsive until just a little while ago. I didn't know if she would be okay or not. She needs to rest and get fully charged. After that we can determine if she will return to normal. I thought you should know something. I think she'll be alright, but only time will tell." Robert had to be honest with him.

"Thank you so much Robert. It's good to at least know something! The imagination tends to go wild not knowing anything. Can I come visit her?" Mack asked hopefully.

"You could, but right now, there's not much to see. She's in sleep and repair mode. The babies are temporarily hooked up to external tanks until we can determine that Betty is well enough to function properly on her own. I know it's hard Mack. Take care of yourself. You know she's in good hands. Bye-bye." He sighed, wishing he had more news to share.

Betty took a long time to recover and was on bed rest for a couple of weeks. Her programs and software finally enabled her to get back to normal functioning for carrying the babies. Essentially, she was like a G-3 right now, in the aspect that she wasn't very mobile. Her equilibrium was a bit off, but she ended up fine-tuning her balance again, so she could walk without fear of falling. Once she no longer needed the external filtration and nutrient systems, she went back to having her own internal tanks in operation.

Mack came to visit Caring Corp. every day during her recovery, not wanting to leave her side ever again. Together, they watched the babies' progress via the ultrasound scans.

Meg and Tom finally came to visit. Meg was now visibly showing her baby bump. Betty was so happy to see her.

Meg pulled up a chair next to Betty's bedside. "How are you feeling, Betty? What an ordeal you went through! Now for a change, you are the patient who's getting cared for. I'm so very sorry I wasn't there for you, like you've always been for me. Did anyone tell you what had happened and why it was that we were not available?" Betty shook her head no.

"We had our phones off, but of course, it was the one time you actually needed us! Unbelievable." Meg felt bad not being there for Betty and related what happened on her last flight.

"Another older businessman had a heart attack! I so wish you had been there. Things might have turned out differently."

Meg recounted tearfully, "We lost him, Betty! Dawn and I worked on him for like an hour, but he didn't pull through. I was so upset. I had never seen anyone die before, right in front of me. I see why you didn't like hospice. And I wasn't even close to this man! Still, I just couldn't stop thinking about it. I was so sad. Tom and I just turned everything off and went to spend some quality time together. It was really rough."

Betty took Meg's hand in hers, "I'm so sorry! I know how you feel, Meg. I do." She looked down sadly. "It is very hard."

"I decided, I'm not going back to work at Quality First anymore. I would eventually have to stop sometime anyway when the baby comes. Daddy is okay with it." She smiled and affectionately imitated Jasper with her voice lowered saying, "Anything that makes you happy Meg."

"It's just that, after going through my kidnapping, the businessman not making it, and then you, my very best friend nearly dying, I need a break and some quiet time away from work. Daddy says I always did take after Momma, preferring a quiet life. Give me family and friends any day. I've had enough career excitement to last a lifetime." Meg rubbed Betty's hand.

"You should rest up too Meg. You've been through a lot." Betty added, "To compound things, as I was trying to seek help, Caring Corp. had an emergency and sweet Rosy, a G-4 made shortly after me, tried to help with restarting a generator and died. Isn't there a saying that deaths occur in threes?"

She shook her head in disbelief. "After my kidnapping, I'm just lucky to still be alive! It's sad for the businessman and Rosy. But I very nearly joined them. I literally saw my life flash before my eyes, just as Leela described it before she died."

"Well Meg," Betty said with a sigh, "the most important thing is that we are both healthy and so are all our children."

Meg thought maybe she misheard, or Betty was tired and what she said didn't come out correctly. Meg smiled at Betty.

"You mean my baby, and we are both healthy?" she clarified.

"Oh my goodness, I was going to tell you, but then I was taken and I hadn't gotten to talk to you since." Betty perked up, and Meg apologized again for not being there.

"No apologies necessary Meg. Listen to me. I had to tell Mack first and then I was going to tell you and Tom right after. We're both going to be mothers. Together!" Betty beamed.

Meg went to hug her but stopped as she thought about it.

"But, how?" Meg looked at Betty raising an eyebrow.

"No, not that way!" Betty giggled. "That is kind of impossible for us. It's a long story if you have the time."

Chapter 13

Fate

The twins were now twelve weeks along. Robert found out that his father had ordered an amniocentesis test to make certain the babies were thriving and had no health issues.

Fetuses shed cells directly into the amniotic fluid, and one of the benefits of the artificial womb was that the test could easily be done, simply by taking a sample from the filtration system when it was drained. Robert wanted to take a look at this test, because he had a hunch. He printed out the results.

Betty saw he had test results and asked how they were.

"As far as the tests go, the wee little ones are doing just splendidly. There was something else I wanted to look at to confirm. See this paper? It shows their DNA. You and I are so much alike sometimes. Curiosity gets the better of us both. Perhaps I'm just a bad influence on you." They both laughed.

Robert went over to the Skin Division, where they cultured semi-organic skin for the models, prosthetics and skin grafting sheets, as well as hair patches, and tissue-based 3-D bioprinted organs and body parts such as the outer ear for transplants. He needed the help of a geneticist that would know about DNA.

When he got there, a new geneticist was working in the lab named Dr. Carvey. She was an intellectual type, who looked the part with glasses, and had her bright red hair tied back in a bun.

It was five minutes before her quitting time, and she was about ready to leave. Robert approached her to talk about reading DNA. He was taken by her beauty and became a bit tongue tied. Being shy around women, he tried to regain his composure.

She's a colleague! You're not proposing, he told himself.

He asked if she might be interested in helping out on a special project. She saw his name tag and her jaw dropped.

"You're Dr. Robert Kerring!" She was star-struck. The two of them were awkwardly stammering as they walked together for her to go clock out, when Dr. Kenneth Kerring came along.

He was surprised to see his son away from his work and appearing to be idly chatting, especially with a young woman.

"What is going on Robert? Don't you have work to do?"

Then, Dr. Kerring realized, *Oh! He's talking causally with a woman around his own age. I have never seen him do that before. I should go fix my blunder and then leave them alone.*

He returned to them saying, "I guess you really are busy. Carry on!" It still didn't come out at all like he meant it to.

Now this thoroughly embarrassed Robert. He visibly blushed and excused himself. He would have to try again later to request help. How was he to speak intelligibly now?

"Dr. Robert Kerring?" she called to him. "I'd love to be involved in the special project. Please give me a chance."

He stopped in his tracks, slowly turned around and came back, his hands tucked up inside the sleeves of his lab coat like a turtle shrinks into its shell. "Really?" She nodded yes.

She reached out her right hand and introduced herself as Dr. Kelly Carvey, and he shook her hand. Robert understood now what Betty meant by having her processors tickle when she was first around Mack. Robert's heart fluttered in the same way, and he became thoroughly smitten with Dr. Carvey. It appeared that it was very mutual.

They agreed they could call each other by their first names, so they were now off to a less awkward start. Robert opened up, explaining what it was he was trying to examine.

They easily related to each other, speaking the same kind of language—the super shy, intellectual type. Some couples may have first dates consisting of meeting for coffee and doughnuts. Intellectuals tend to do scholarly projects together.

Robert met Kelly at the Skin Division at 5:30 p.m. after the workday was over. They drove over to his robotics lab in a golf cart. On the way, he explained that he was mainly interested in looking at the strands of DNA from the amniocentesis, their letter sequences, and their complementary strings. He said he thought he remembered seeing a similar combination before, but he needed the help of an expert geneticist. She smiled shyly.

They arrived at his robotics lab, where he had kept the singed notepaper that he had written down Betty's unique coding from when he tried to examine it, before the computer caught fire. After that happened, Dr. Kerring had forbidden him to do any more code examination on Betty herself, but he never said that he couldn't look at what he already had.

They compared the DNA sequences of the amniocentesis to his written notes from Betty's unique coding. To their surprise, half of the letter sequences exactly matched that of the DNA of both the babies. It appeared Robert's hunch was correct! He thanked Kelly for her help but thought a minute.

"Would you like to meet Betty Fourré Schwartz? She is like my adoptive sister and is convalescing in her old dorm room. Oh, that probably sounds very weird that a caregiver model is like my sister." He looked down, feeling awkward.

"Not at all! I have always admired Betty and wished I could get to meet her in person. I had no idea she was here. Wow! It would be such an honor!" Kelly smiled at him.

They came to Betty's room. Robert knocked on her door.

"Sis, are you up?" He slowly came into the room.

"Robbie! Betty said. "You told me not to pick you up and twirl you around, so I'm staying right here." She patted her legs.

"I have someone I want you to meet. This is Dr. Kelly Carvey. She's a geneticist in the Skin Division."

Betty looked at her and Robert. Both exhibited similar body language and lack of eye contact. She could read them, much like she read Tom and Meg. She got a huge smile, and vigorously shook Kelly's hand. "Very, very nice to meet you Dr. Carvey!"

Robert could tell Betty was reading him, and she saw he

liked Kelly. He frowned and put his finger up to his mouth to shush her, but of course, Betty was an incurable romantic.

"Robbie, there's nothing wrong with liking her 'like that.'"

"What's with you and Dad?" he retorted and almost started to leave the room, but realized, he'd brought Kelly himself.

He sighed, and Kelly was looking down, visibly smiling. Betty whispered to her, "That goes both ways you know."

"Alright Betty, can we please be serious?" Robert said.

"Well, I really was being serious, but you two should do the same. I can read you both like a book." Betty grinned.

"I like her Robbie," Betty said very matter-of-factly.

Kelly broke out laughing. "You guys are so funny together; I just love this. You are so much like a brother and sister. I should know, I have eleven siblings. Betty, you are just like the heroine I always pictured. Thank you for making things less awkward. I've always been very shy too."

"What just happened?" Robert wasn't sure, but it seemed like Betty had made everything better. Then he thought about it. *Oh, being serious, as with relationships. I get it now.*

"Alright Betty, I do have a very serious question for you."

She looked up at him and smiled. "Yes Robbie?"

"When you added the new coding after I gave you the ability to override your original core programming. How exactly did you do it? I mean, what did you do, and how did you come up with what you were supposed to add?"

He pulled up two chairs, motioning that Kelly could sit down too, and they could listen and take notes.

"I told you Robbie, I can't recall it at all. It's almost like there is something blocking my memory in that area. I'll try to answer as best I can." She stared ahead thinking back to then.

"I remember looking at myself in a mirror and reversing the image, just as though I were someone else who was looking at me. And I was thinking, 'What were you like, person with my original face?' I didn't know her, and I had no idea that Mack or Miri existed yet. You told me about Miri a few years later when I asked how it was that I got my specific face."

"I remember when you asked how your face was chosen." Robert nodded, then said to Kelly, "The G-4s' facial identities are chosen randomly from the Social Security Death Index."

Betty continued, "I just stared at the being in the mirror and went into this trance-like state right when I was inserting the new coding. It was strange, and highly irresponsible of me! It was as if someone else was writing the code as I inserted it, but I can no longer access it. As soon as I stopped, I got an alert 'Access Denied' and I stopped trying. After that, I became conscious. I mean, really conscious! Then, I started developing real human-like emotions, and I have not been able to prevent them ever since. Does that answer your question, Robbie?"

"Yes, you did great Betty," he reassured her. Kelly sat there quietly observing it all, not wanting to interrupt them.

"Here's the thing. Dad told me to drop it, so I can't look directly into your coding anymore. But from what I saw of your special code that day I investigated it, the letters looked so much like DNA, it really made me wonder. I was just comparing your coding I wrote down to the DNA of your babies. Half of the sequences match, just as though you were their real mother!"

"Are you saying, my special coding is actually Miri's DNA?" Betty stared at him. "How is that even possible?"

Robert put both of his hands up and then shrugged his shoulders saying, "I have no idea, Betty. That is what piqued my curiosity so much. I have never seen anything like it. I wish I had a sample of something organic that was Miri's. We would know for sure. I highly suspect that your special coding does match her DNA. But that would be too bizarre for words."

He shook his head. "Had I not seen it myself, I'd normally say it's totally impossible for your computer brain to have anything other than 1s and 0s. That's what all computer code is made up of. It is binary! But with you? There has been nothing anyone could call 'normal,'" Robert said, making air quotes.

Betty felt a combination of happiness and wonderment.

"Can we tell this to Mack? I knew by carrying his children I was considered their mother in that respect, but could I somehow really be, Miri now? But how, and who had me insert the DNA coding, and why was I in a trance-like state?"

"We should talk to him. I'm wondering if he could get a

sample of Miri's DNA somehow. An old toothbrush or comb with some of her hair? That would be the proof we would need," Robert said excitedly, raising his eyebrows.

Betty and Robert told Mack about it all. Mack agreed to give them something of Miri's: a ponytail. She had cut her hair after growing it long, so she could make a wig from it. Of course, Mack saved it. He sealed it in an airtight bag and stored in the closet. It was preserved perfectly with no degradation.

Robert took some strands of hair from it, got it tested, and the DNA was a perfect match to Betty's code on his paper!

Kelly was stunned and said, "It's Divine Providence!"

Betty jumped in, "That is exactly what Mack says in Hebrew, 'Hashgacha Pratit!'"

"Well, I don't know about that," Robert muttered.

Both Betty and Kelly shot him a look as to question him.

"What?" He shrugged. "I've never really known quite what to believe. But don't bring the subject up to Dad, he says he's an Atheist. I know he took Mom and April's deaths personally."

Betty shook her head, "I feel sad for Dad at times. I just don't understand, how you men of science can see miracles happen every day, and not believe in some higher power. After all, if I was made by you, my creators, why couldn't there be some sort of higher power that made you?"

Robert said, "Well, after all these coincidences, you may have me convinced. I can't explain any of it. I'm not used to that!"

Chapter 14
Eyewitness

Betty stayed at Caring Corp. to convalesce for a total of about three weeks, until it was finally determined that she was completely back to normal and could safely function and support the babies. Mack came daily, overnighting when he could, and stayed on weekends. Betty's dorm room had a temporary set up for Mack with a cot, plus a mini fridge, hotplate, and microwave, so he could at least prepare and eat food.

Betty's balance was fine now, and her batteries kept a steady charge. All functions had been tested rigorously, and were working normally, both for Betty and for the babies. The fetuses were now over thirteen weeks along, and Betty was just barely starting to show a baby bump. Being much like a large, thick bag beneath the skin, ectogenesis pods were flexible and expansive. The twins would later fill it out, and Betty would look just like any other normal, pregnant woman.

Caring Corp. was very secure, so she had been safe there since nobody outside of the campus had known of her existence apart from Meg and Tom. All employees mandatorily had to sign a Non-Disclosure Agreement concerning anything that went on at Caring Corp. She had been isolated during her convalescence, so not all employees even knew she was there.

Betty's life would be in danger if Gio would ever find out

that she had survived and could identify him. Mack and Betty discussed the possibility of witness protection or relocating at the least. They decided to prepare accordingly. Mack wrapped up the last of his cases in Des Moines but hadn't told his mother about Betty's kidnapping. She was still recovering from a major operation herself, and he didn't want to make her worry.

Mack thought it would be a good idea to contact his old friend Special Agent Woodrow Everett, better known to most people as "Woody". He might be able to advise them as to what was the best thing to do, since it was his specialty.

Mack and Woody had both attended high school together in Baltimore, Maryland, and later studied law together in college, but then they both decided on different career paths.

It was quite an interesting friendship, as they were total opposites. Aside from judicial trials, Mack was on the quiet side. Being a creature of habit, he preferred to have a regular schedule and less surprises. He wanted to help people defend their civil rights. It wasn't very glamorous, didn't always pay well, and some might even consider it a bit boring.

Mack's friend Woody, on the other hand, was far more outgoing. He loved the unpredictability and action of proactively fighting crime and putting criminals away. He rose in ranks in the FBI to become a Special Agent, as he did what he loved.

Mack got in touch with Woody. They scheduled to meet

with Betty at Caring Corp. It was the safest place for them, and they were a bit concerned as to what to do and how to proceed.

Woody came to the office asking for Mack. Dr. Kerring escorted him in a golf cart throughout the facility, until they reached Betty's room. He announced the visitor then left.

"Woody!" Mack came out to greet him.

"Mack! It's been a long time!" They hugged and patted each other's backs. "I haven't seen you since Miri's funeral!"

"And you must be Betty. Oh gosh, you look just like Miri, it's astounding! You have a very different voice than hers though, a bit lower. Wow, I've heard and seen so much about you. You're an all-American hero! It's so nice to finally meet you!"

"And you as well," Betty nodded and smiled. Since her kidnapping, she decided not to hug any new unrelated men anymore like she used to. She could tell it bothered Mack.

"So, Betty, you are really a bot?" Woody looked her over.

"Yes, but we prefer to be called 'man-mades' or 'models.' I do have official personhood, and I have . . . ."

"Semi-organic living skin," Mack said, chuckling as he finished her sentence along with her. Betty smiled at him.

"You know Mack, I have been following you both on social media, and in the news." Woody informed him.

"But I don't really do social media," Mack replied.

"My point exactly! Anytime I hear your name, it perks my ears up and I listen. For a quiet guy, you sure do know how to get attention, and in your current situation, that's not good!"

"I know Woody, but what should we do? Can we get into witness protection? Betty is already thought to be dead, at least by Giovanni Marino. If she stays that way, she should be safe. But what about me? Would we both be eligible?"

Betty asked, cocking her head, "Isn't Mack in danger too by association? I did witness Gio and his warehouse, I even filmed a lot of it and stored it in my account in the cloud."

Woody looked at Betty. "You got video footage of his operation? We have been trying to get someone into his narcotics lab for years, but he has a very close-knit crew. Most of his people are relatives, or friends of relatives."

"Melissa Cosbie was related to Gio?" Betty asked.

"Our CI said she was the girlfriend of a nephew of Marino's, Antonio Rossi a.k.a. 'Four-Finger Tony' after an encounter he had with one of Gio's enemies. Can you show me the video?"

"I'll download it. There's a monitor over here." She pointed.

Betty started staring into space as she started downloading and concentrating on sending the video footage to the monitor.

"She does this often?" He pointed to her staring into space.

"Yes, whenever she is concentrating or in deep thought. Basically, she is processing information," Mack answered.

"I can relate," Woody said. "I tend to space out when I concentrate. Now I know just what to call it! To 'Betty-out.'"

Mack laughed. "That's so true, to 'Betty-out,' ha-ha-ha!"

The footage came on the monitor now. Betty was traveling through the warehouse, being carried by Leo and Alfred.

"Did you smell anything unusual as you were going through the warehouse, Betty?" Woody asked. "Maybe similar to ammonia or rotten eggs?

"I do not smell in the same manner that humans do, but I can analyze the molecular structures of chemical compounds in the air. Normally, I can detect unsafe levels of toxins, such as carbon monoxide, hydrogen sulfide, methane, propane, natural gas, and radon gas. But I had these functions turned off to conserve power. If I detect them, my programming causes me to automatically let out an alert tone. I'll demonstrate!"

A message sounded in her head, *"Test alarm initiated."*

Betty then let out an airhorn-like sound from her mouth. Mack and Woody covered their ears with their hands, frowning.

She noticed her demonstration was causing them discomfort, so she halted the test alarm function. A message went off in her head, *"Test aborted."*

"I'm so sorry!" she said, covering her mouth with her hand, getting slightly embarrassed. She had only projected the sound outward but shielded the babies from hearing it as much as possible, so that they wouldn't become startled or frightened.

"Really, at the time, I was just trying to get a sense of where I was, and to be able to be found. It was a huge old building. I remember they said it was on Central Avenue. I heard a lot of fans going, big industrial ones. I didn't know what I was recording, I saw there were windows way up toward the extra-high ceilings, but I couldn't see out. I didn't want to use more power than I had to at the time. I had very little left in reserve."

She merely had opened her eyes and kept them opened as she was recording but did get parts of the drug manufacturing operation as she was carried through. There were sheets of plastic dividing areas, people in protective suits and gas masks, test tubes on tables, and bins full of crystalline powders.

"This is awesome, Betty! But wait, can you stop it and zoom in on that figure in the corner?" Woody asked, as he pointed to something on the screen with a distinctive shape.

"Sure, do you need me to go back?" Betty had control over all the video features. She zoomed in on the figure in the corner. "Is this it?" She held the video in place and zoomed in closely. "I can zoom to microscopic level, if needed," she said proudly.

"That's it." Woody looked closer. "No way! That is what I thought I saw. This statue of an angel with a sword was taken from the Guardian Angel Casino in Las Vegas, Nevada owned by the Leonis, who are a rival crime family."

"Really!" Betty was surprised. She didn't realize she had gotten something other than her general surroundings.

"We suspected that the Marinos were trying to set up shop there in Las Vegas as well. Rumor has it that the Lioni family killed Giovanni's father, and they were trying to keep the

Marinos out of the area. They didn't want more competition."

Woody pointed at the angel with the sword on the monitor.

"This famous statue was a tourist attraction at their casino. It was reported stolen, and nobody knew of its whereabouts. Marino must have been holding onto it for leverage all this time. Wow Betty, this would be enough to start a major war between the crime families. I mean, the drug operation in itself is huge. But this is information only you would know about and could provide. It's very valuable, and I think you do have grounds for going into a witness relocation program. The bureau can help set you both up in a new location at the least."

Woody added, "You might be interested to know, that when they found you in the river Betty, they also found another body at the same time. It too was wrapped in chain and attached to blocks in the same exact way. Obviously, another victim of Marino's. We identified the body, and it was a CI who was working within his organization, getting close to the drug operation. A crying shame, he was a very good man who helped us a lot. We couldn't release the details of course. His family members could be in danger if it was known. These are extremely dangerous people we're dealing with."

Betty investigated the meaning and related it all out loud:

"'CI.' Definition: Abbreviation for 'confidential informant.'"

"So, a 'CI' is a person working undercover to assist law enforcement to gather information about crime or criminals to be able to prosecute a perpetrator. Very admirable. That's so sad." Betty looked down. "I know how dangerous they can be."

"While we were driving, I tried to get some sort of reading on the van I was in and tap into cell phones, but there was no sign of anything there at all! I must really be slipping to not be able to find any signal," Betty said concerned.

"No, you aren't Betty," Woody reassured her. "Giovanni Marino has technophobia. According to our CI, he ordered his people specifically to not carry or use cellphones and made them get rid of any GPS units in their cars, trucks, or vans. He is totally paranoid about 'Big Brother' watching everyone and has made every attempt to avoid technology that can be traced, tracked, or hacked into. He is always watching his back, and extremely hard to pin anything on."

"Oh, that does explain it." Betty nodded thoughtfully.

"I mean, you probably saw the ransom note. It was just plain, old-fashioned typed-on paper. Whoever did it must have used gloves, we couldn't get any prints from it, and your gold medal was wiped clean too. No hand-written note that could be analyzed. And something we often see, no collection of glued-on magazine or newspaper clippings to say certain words. I always find those the most humorous because fingerprints are so easy to get from them."

"That makes sense," Betty acknowledged.

Mack wondered, "So Woody, you say the information

wasn't released on the other body that was found? Your CI? Was there anything at all released to the public?"

"After a thorough consult with the bureau, we advised the local police to tell the press that two bodies were discovered in the Hudson River. One was unidentified, and the other was Single Act of Heroism Citizen Honors Award winner, Betty Fourré Schwartz. Also, we told them to say the bodies were discovered two days later than when you were rescued, just to make sure Marino thought you were dead. It took that long to identify the CI's body anyway," Woody explained. "There wasn't much left of him, but dental records proved his identity, despite several missing teeth in the front. Poor guy. He must have been severely tortured. It doesn't go well for people who cross Giovanni Marino."

"No doubt it was done in the 'special room' in the basement where they held me captive," Betty reflected.

"There were all kinds of human bodily fluids on the floor and all over the tools hanging on the wall. I saw it with my ultraviolet vision mode. It was terrifying!"

"That could have very likely happened to you if he knew you could identify him. In that respect, you're lucky you were only dumped in the river and not slowly tortured to death." Woody and Mack looked at each other, and back at Betty.

"It sounds like you guys took every precaution possible to protect Betty. That is so appreciated," Mack said relieved.

"But what should the two of us be doing next? Anything?"

"Just sit tight here for now guys. This is a very safe and secure place, temporarily anyway. It was very fortunate that the Kerrings brought you here," Woody observed.

"I couldn't have recuperated better anywhere else," Betty said. "I mean, this is basically the only hospital location in the country for Caring Corp. models. Any injured models are automatically shipped here to be cared for, and then once they pass their diagnostic and physical tests for good health, they get shipped back out again."

"So, tell me Betty, I'm just curious. What makes you so much different from all the other caregiver models? It seems almost like trouble follows you!" Woody wondered.

"You could say I'm considered special. Not just since I was the first G-4 prototype, but Dr. Robert Kerring tweaked my coding to allow me to override my original base code to gain more knowledge and make independent decisions. It was an experiment, and only done to me. None of my other G-4 model sisters ever got this enhancement. I further did something else which I do not recall, that gave me human emotions.

"Wow, that is all amazing Betty," Woody replied. "And you got Miri's old face too. Whew, no wonder Mack is so much in love with you. I can see it in his eyes." Woody smiled and nudged Mack playfully with his elbow as Mack looked down smiling bashfully. "Between your hero status, and your uniqueness, we have got to protect you!"

Chapter 15
A Time to Move On

"We're so grateful for your help in protecting us Woody," Betty added. "But there's one little wrinkle in this whole thing."

"Umm . . ." Mack knew where she was going with this. "Actually, there are two little wrinkles?" He smiled ear to ear.

"True, we're going to have to think about them too." Betty and Mack just sat there smiling at each other and looking into each other's eyes with the most content and loving expressions.

"Should you tell him, or should I?" Mack asked Betty.

"Well, he's your old friend, maybe you should tell him. I need to get used to being less sociable with men where you want us to go." Betty stated.

"Very good point," Mack agreed. "I'm so proud of you."

"So, Woody. It turns out that we have new additions on the way," he blurted out. "We'll have to worry about keeping them protected too! It isn't just going to be the two of us." Mack pointed back and forth at himself and Betty.

"What do you mean Mack?" Woody looked puzzled. "Who else do you want to bring along, and why? Your mother? I thought she lived in Iowa. She shouldn't be of interest to Gio."

"No, it's not my mother," Mack grinned with a faraway look, then looked at Betty with a sweet smile.

"Oh alright. It's our future children!" Betty announced proudly, as she rubbed her small but noticeable baby bump.

"Mack, you're going to be a father? That's great news! But wait a minute! If Betty is a model, how does that even work?"

"Betty was the one who arranged it all, and she surprised me with it." Mack smiled happily.

Woody laughed. "She arranged it? Now you really have some explaining to do! You weren't involved? So, you're not really the father. I'm still a bit confused."

"Oh, I am definitely their father, and my late wife Miri was their mother. Frozen twin embryos from the Fertility Center." Mack motioned toward the direction of that building.

"I understand now, it's something that's carefully controlled. In that case, I should wish you a Mazal Tov!" Woody grinned.

Mack nodded, and Woody started dancing around with him in circles, singing, "Siman Tov, U'Mazal Tov." They kept repeating the song over and over as they danced arm in arm around the room in circles, both shouting, "hey!" now and then.

Betty was thoroughly amused. She had never seen Mack behave this way. He was almost a different person around Woody, more relaxed and spontaneous. She did remember reading in some of his psychology books about when old friends had grown up together and then later reunited, their behavior would often revert back to how they acted together when they were younger.

It's really just an interesting psychological phenomenon, she thought to herself, smiling as she watched them.

Woody stopped dancing and became a bit more serious. "Wow, we really do have a lot of catching up to do my friend. For sure, we need to protect Betty, but the babies may put a bit of a clinker in things. Do you have any idea where you would like to go?" Woody asked with a look of concern.

Mack thought about it very hard and stared into space as if to "Betty-out", as was Woody's newly invented phrase.

"It should ideally be some place with a large Orthodox Jewish population. I can't think of a safer place, because the Orthodox community is generally more isolated. Most secular activity is frowned upon. Many people don't watch television, and some don't even use the internet. Others have kosher phones that don't do anything but call and receive texts. Any strangers that don't fit in are looked at as potential threats, so I don't think Giovanni's people would stand a chance at trying to infiltrate the neighborhood. Most non-Jews don't have a clue about the Orthodox way of life, which is fine with the community. What about our old teenage stomping grounds in Baltimore?" Mack asked with a hopeful tone.

Woody shrugged his mouth, narrowing his eyebrows as he listened to Mack's reasoning. He had to make sure they would remain safe, and it would be a wise decision for them to be going there. After thinking a few minutes, he shook his head no.

"Normally, we would never agree to having witnesses be relocated to a place where they want to go. Someone is bound to recognize them there," Woody commented. "No matter where it is, or will be, it must be kept a complete secret. We'll have to find a rabbi in the new place who can keep everything confidential. There's no going back to your old rabbi."

"I understand," Mack said. "Unless there is something considered detrimental to others, rabbis generally do keep things confidential, so that shouldn't be a problem at all."

"I'll run it by some people at the bureau and see what they say, but I can't guarantee it will be in Baltimore. Only that it will be in an Orthodox community, somewhere."

Mack explained, "Me, and some of the more Modern Orthodox people of the community do have contact with the outside world, usually due to our occupations. We're not quite as isolated from modern-day life as the Amish after all, except maybe on Shabbat," Mack added with a chuckle.

"But really, for the most part, given the amount of exposure Betty has had, it still would probably be the safest place, aside from Caring Corp. Unless you think we should just stay here in hiding for the rest of our lives. That's really no way to live though." Mack shook his head and continued.

"You see, nobody ever knew Miri in Baltimore, we flew Rabbi Fried out to Cincinnati to officiate at our wedding where she lived, and then we moved to Albany. I figured, if I went back to Baltimore, who would really remember a quiet, unpopular teenage boy from like, twenty-five years earlier. Boys tend to change pretty much over that amount of time. I think the only person who would remember me is Rabbi and Rebbetzin Fried. They were rather young themselves when he took over as the congregational rabbi of the synagogue."

Woody sighed. "Alright, I'll see what I can do, but don't count on it. Wherever it will be, we'll have to get you both IDs. You shouldn't need new Social Security numbers. We may be able to get a law degree issued with the new name. I don't know for sure. I need to consult the higher ups."

Woody got some pictures of them with his phone.

"It's highly unusual, but if there's anyone very close to you, we can't have them stirring up suspicion by trying to look for you. Most people don't get the chance, but if you must let them know you're leaving, they have to be trusted to keep it a complete secret. Otherwise, they need to believe you're dead or missing." Woody cautioned. "What about new names?"

"Can I use my Hebrew name?" Mack asked. "It might be better for fitting in, and then just change the last name."

"How different is it, Mack?" Woody looked doubtful.

"Michael ben Moshe, so how about, 'Michael Gold'? Gold was Miri's maiden name," Mack stated. She was the only child of older parents, and they both are gone, so the 'Gold' surname was pretty much forgotten, sad to say."

Woody thought about it. "Normally we discourage the use of maiden names as a policy, but yes, I think in your case that should work. It's not your own mother's maiden name. I had forgotten about that, thinking your Hebrew name was Maccabee, but that's really your legal name, right?"

Mack nodded yes and said, "That is correct."

"How do you know so much about Hebrew names Woody?" Betty questioned. "Even I know only a little bit."

"I have a Hebrew name. It's 'Yehuda,'" he whispered. "My mother's Jewish, but my father wasn't. Orthodox people consider me Jewish since Mom is. Sometimes, I'd go to Mack's synagogue, or shul, as they call it, for special events. It's not like I wasn't welcome there. I just had other, different interests. I had, and still have a hard time sitting still for a three-hour long Shabbat service."

Betty raised her hand as if she were in class. "Yehuda, I know what I want my name to be!" she chirped happily.

"I've only allowed one person in my life to ever call me by my Hebrew name." He frowned. "I still prefer Woody!"

"I'm sorry, Woody." Betty nodded. "I understand. 'Miriam Elizabeth Gold,' and 'Miriam Elisheva' as my Hebrew name."

"Aw Betty, that's so sweet. I'd have thought you would want to step out of Miri's shadow for once. But you really want to take her whole name?" Mack was amazed at her unselfishness. "You are so special. I love you so much."

"Uhem, guys?" Woody tried to get the lovebirds back on

track. "That works Betty. Exactly why did you choose it?"

"I analyzed all the facts and did several simulations. The most successful one indicated that if we are going to be in a Jewish community using previously established Hebrew names, it would be normal and accepted. Mack has pictures from his wedding, and I look exactly like Miri. As far as anyone would know, we're just an already-married couple moving to a new neighborhood. His old identity is the perfect new identity! Our whole history is already in place." She thought it was ingenious.

"Mack has Miri's and his Jewish marriage contract hanging on the wall in the living room," she told Woody.

"Yes, it's a decorative copy of the Ketuba in a frame. You're right Betty, this could really work! You're going to have to learn the ins and outs of Orthodox Judaism though. You know some, but I'll have to teach you more to get you ready."

"Sounds like a plan guys. Very good!" Woody patted Mack on the back. "I'll have to get used to calling you Michael now, but very important! Do not let anyone else know your new names. Practice in private, but don't tell anyone else. I know you've had a few friends visit you here already, but if they were to slip up and reveal your new identities to others, it could put you in grave danger," Woody cautioned.

"I'll get working on your paperwork and all that goes with it. You can arrange a goodbye party here. I think Caring Corp. is still the most secure and safe place you could be for now. But for your children's sake, you must seamlessly blend into the Orthodox community to make your new life work."

"And Mack, or, 'Michael' is right. Get learning 'Miriam Elisheva!' " Woody smiled and got ready to leave. He had a lot of preliminary work to do. "Are you able to forward all that video footage to us at the FBI?"

"Sure Woody, just tell me where to send it."

He wrote down a web address and his email on a paper he tore out of the little notebook he always carried with him.

"Perfect. That is great evidence we can be working with. Maybe someday you can return to your normal life if we can get Marino on something. He's nearly untouchable since he uses other people to do all his illegal dirty work."

Betty added, "I did manage to get coordinates for the warehouse from my GPS just as we were leaving for the river. I sent it to the cloud. I couldn't get anything from being in the basement and couldn't transmit underwater either. I also heard a train nearby. I'll send you the coordinates too."

Woody stopped and thought a minute. "You know, you would be a very valuable asset if you ever worked with the FBI. What other talents do you have?"

Betty thought a few seconds and started rattling off some of her more notable features. "Of course, since I scan and record everything, I literally have a photographic memory. I can text, call, and phone people in my mind without uttering a sound. Depending on the system, I can communicate with other computers and persuade them to let me into them, but only for a good cause! Never to steal or harm. Just want to make that perfectly clear!" She wagged her finger.

"It's a shame you need to be in hiding." Woody frowned.

"I can speak over one-hundred different languages, plus American Sign Language that I learned myself. It wasn't programed in originally. I can read micro-expressions, voice intonations and body language to tell if someone is lying. My vision can be utilized to see in several different spectrums of light, such as X-ray, ultraviolet, infrared, and of course normal visible light, and I can zoom from nearly telescopic to almost microscopic levels. My enhanced hearing frequencies are up to slightly over sixty-eight thousand hertz. I am a certified registered nurse and medical caregiver, as well as now being a certified paralegal, just to name a few things."

"Wow, such a waste of potential! You're like a detective extraordinaire with a whole, built-in crime lab!" Woody was quite impressed. Betty became very excited at that idea.

"But Betty, there's a very important issue to realize," Mack said. "Not to burst your bubble, but for one thing, it could be dangerous, and for another, you aren't able to defend yourself!" Mack looked at Woody. "That's her only programming flaw."

Woody sighed. "Too bad. Well, let's keep making plans. I'll get everything arranged at the bureau and get back with you, or better yet, Dr. Kerring?" They all nodded in agreement.

Mack added, "I need to contact whoever our rabbi will be and let him know what is going on. He'll be our direct link for getting into the community. When I last called Rabbi Fried, I asked about civil marriage to Betty. Things have gotten quite a bit more complicated since then." Mack pointed at Betty's belly. "Whoever do we get, maybe he can help find us a place to stay until we get settled into a place of our own."

"This is so exciting! Right guys?" Betty said, speaking toward the babies in her tummy.

Woody waved goodbye. "See you later, Michael and Miriam! You two start getting used to using those new names now, at least between each other. It must appear completely natural and without thought, or your covers could be blown. You might also think about trying out a new look."

"Thank you for everything Woody. We will practice," Mack and Betty both said in unison.

"Michael? Oh, this is weird. Do you think I should dye my hair? Maybe you should grow a beard." Betty agreed that they should be a bit less recognizable anyway.

"That might be a very good idea, Miriam. I'm so used to saying Miri, that Miram isn't so much of a stretch. You should be able to reprogram from Mack to Michael, no?"

She nodded. "It's just a matter of word replacement. But I'm so fond of calling you Mack." She looked at him sweetly.

Chapter 16
Going Green

"I'm calling Meg. I don't think there's danger in tracking calls or texts since they originate in my highly encrypted mind."

"Hi Meg? I have a lot to tell you, but perhaps you could get me a package of blonde hair dye. We could be twins!"

"Sure Betty, anything for you. I'll buy some and come over in a few minutes." Meg hung up, went to a nearby grocery and found hair dye, then headed to Caring Corp.

Meg arrived at Caring Corp. and went to Betty's dorm room. "Hi Betty, I'm here for our 'ladies only' event."

"Hi Meg!" Betty came over to hug her, and in the process, their somewhat pronounced tummies touched. They looked down at them and giggled. "We might not be able to reach each other for much longer!"

Betty said, "Robbie's official new girlfriend Dr. Kelly Carvey will be coming a little bit later when she gets done in the lab. She is a geneticist. I like her. She is so much like Robbie. It's a good match!"

"Another successful match made?" Meg grinned.

"I can't take credit for this one. Robbie found her all on his own. I like this getting together with the girls. I guess I do need to start getting used to only hanging around other women where I'm going. Mack says the women stick with the women, and the men stick with the men. It apparently is not seen as proper for women to associate with men. And I certainly can't hug them or touch them in any way."

"Poor Betty, that is going to be very hard for you, isn't it. You're such a hugger!" Meg giggled.

"Oh, I have slowly been getting used to it." Betty sighed.

"So, if you want to be twins, let's cut your hair, then we can dye it." Meg got some scissors and a large towel ready, and then brought over the box of hair dye.

"You washed your hair a day or two ago? It says on the box, by doing that, it allows the dye to adhere to your natural oils. But I thought oil was actually supposed to repel stuff. Hmm."

"I washed it two days ago. Remember, I have no sweat glands or bodily secretions like humans do!" Betty laughed and made a grimacing face. "To tell you the truth, which I have to anyway, I do not think that I have natural oils either," Betty remarked. "I sure hope this works."

"I'm going to miss your beautiful brunette hair. It is so thick and luscious! Some women would kill to have hair as nice as yours." Meg played with Betty's hair running her fingers through it. Then she started trimming Betty's hair to shoulder length like hers, fluffed it and brushed her off well to get rid of any lose hairs, and then started applying the dye.

"It says to let it sit for twenty minutes." Meg noted.

"Okay, sounds good Meg. I'll set my timer." Betty set her internal clock for twenty minutes.

Kelly finally arrived at Betty's room. "Okay ladies, I'm finally here to help. Aw, you started without me!" She looked a bit disappointed and made a pouting face in jest. Then she picked up the box of hair dye Meg had bought, looked at it, and looked closer at Betty's hair, squinting slightly.

"Um, girls?" Kelly noticed that Betty's hair was looking more greenish than blond. "How long before this stuff takes affect? I've never done this kind of thing before, but is this some sort of normal transitionary thing?"

Meg looked closer. "Kelly, I think you may be right. You're the geneticist, could there some kind of counterreaction between her semi-organic hair and the dye?"

"It looks like it. I mean, even her skin is starting to turn green where it was applied! I should contact Dr. Kerring. I'll bet it's some kind of chemical reaction with the Peppergrape extracts infused into the semi-organic skin."

Meg was very embarrassed. "Oh my goodness, Betty, I'm so sorry!"

For all the many times Betty had always been there for her, it seemed like no matter how hard she tried to help Betty, Meg always seemed to mess something up. She felt just terrible. She had turned her best friend green!

Betty had a horrified look. "How am I supposed to blend

in with green hair? Kelly, how long is this going to last?"

Kelly looked at the box. "At the shortest, one month. At longest, two months?" She frowned and clenched her teeth.

"Can it be reversed?" Betty was almost in a panic.

"We could try hydrogen peroxide. We probably should have used that in the first place." Kelly stroked her chin in thought.

"Wow, you look just like Robbie when you think!" Betty burst out giggling.

"Robbie frowns too when he thinks hard," Kelly added.

Meg asked, "You call him Robbie too?" She started giggling as well. Kelly put a finger up to her mouth to shush them, and they all started giggling.

Kelly whispered, "Yes. We've been getting closer lately. He really is very romantic, in a scientific sort of way. They always say, 'watch out for the quiet ones.'" She blushed.

Mack came in hearing all the laughter, and suddenly all three of them looked up at him at the same time and stopped laughing, realizing that Betty had a head full of green hair.

"What have you done now?" Mack came to her and leaned over, resting all his weight on his hands on the arms of the chair that Betty sat in. He looked in her eyes and she gave him a pitiful look. He sighed. "Meg, did you do this?"

"How was I supposed to know that the blonde hair dye would react with her, 'semi-organic living skin?'" And they all started giggling again. Meg and Kelly almost started getting tears in their eyes they had been laughing so hard.

"I think I can fix it," Kelly said. "We'll try the peroxide."

"It isn't going to turn blue or purple next, is it?" Mack said with a worried tone.

Kelly went into her analytical mode. "Her skin contains infusions of Peppergrape. Its close relative Peppervine can cause allergic reactions, so I strongly suspect that it is a chemical interaction due to the Peppergrape. Perhaps, it is oxalic acid present in the infusion within her skin that is what is reacting to the dye. I don't know for sure, but, at worst, if we keep washing at it with peroxide, maybe within a month, or at least six washing cycles, she will at least have blonde hair. That is what we were trying to achieve in the first place."

"Has anyone told you that you talk just like Robert?" Mack said, and they all started laughing. "Should we just put off our exit until her hair grows out, and gets back to normal? Is there a way to speed up the process?"

"Not that I know of Mack," Kelly answered.

"Can I ask a silly question?" Mack said looking at Betty. "Why didn't you just opt for wearing a wig? You would have had to do that anyway in the Orthodox community. Married women typically cover their hair. Well, Ashkenazim, or European Jews, usually use wigs. That would be our custom. Or you could do like Ma does and wear a scarf or snood, or even a hat. She thinks they're more comfortable." Mack shrugged his shoulders and raised his hands.

"I didn't think of that," Betty answered, and felt very silly. That was quite a logical thing to do, and she still could.

"Alright, I guess that is what I'll do then! Back on schedule. Thank you, ladies. If anything, this has been a bonding experience, and a real learning one too. I will never, ever try to dye my hair again! I can tell anyone else that I am allergic to hair dye. And it is very true!"

Preparations for their eventual exit continued, but Betty urged Mack to spend some time with his mother, and to send her love and regards. He arranged for one last flight to Des Moines to break the news to his mother that they had to leave. It was so sad, because here he had just gotten her back, in the state that he remembered her as he was growing up, and now he might not ever get to see her again.

Mack took the plane to Des Moines and closed up shop on his private practice, returning the keys to the owner of the building. Then he made the trip to the nursing home to see his mother. He signed in and went to her apartment, arrived, and knocked on the door.

"Maccabee!" Mrs. Schwartz greeted him with a warm hug. "So nice to see you. Where is Miri? I was hoping she would come with you regularly from now on. I'll get some cookies and make some tea."

She went to her kitchenette to put on the kettle.

"Come on in and sit down with me." She patted a chair.

"Thanks Ma." Mack kind of sniffled, thinking sadly that this might be his last trip here.

"What's the matter Mack? Are you getting a cold?" His mother felt his forehead for a temperature.

"I'm fine, Ma. I just have quite a few things to tell you. But first, how are you doing?"

She smiled at Mack, her eyes twinkling with happiness.

"I'm doing splendidly! My memory is back to normal, and I no longer have those horrid headaches. I am so grateful to Miri. It was like a veil was lifted from my head. I barely remember some of the past few years, they are kind of foggy. When I do recall some of my interactions with people, I wonder to myself, 'Now why did I do or say that? Why couldn't I remember something so simple?' But really, it has been a difference of night and day. I still do not understand how I could not recognize you, my very own son on some occasions. I feel just terrible about that."

"Aw, it's okay, Ma. Pressure on the brain from the tumor can cause all sorts of unusual results. The important thing is that you're better now and can function normally again. It's so good to have you back!" He smiled.

"It is so good to be back. Miri told me that at the hospital, I was asking for your father sometimes. How could I not have remembered that he passed?" She put her hand to her cheek and shook her head. "I'm so embarrassed."

"Don't be Ma. The mind often forgets traumatic things."

The kettle started whistling, and she returned with her tray of cookies, the pot, and cups, setting them down on the coffee table. She poured him a cup of tea and handed it to him. "What do you need to tell me Mack?"

"Well Ma, there's good news and bad news. Which would you like to hear first?"

"Brace me with the bad news first," she said with a sigh. "I always like to save the best for last."

Mack wondered what he should tell her. He wanted to tell her the truth but couldn't tell her everything. She mustn't be put in a position where she could slip up and talk about their situation. With her always having been honest to a fault, he couldn't see her ever lying to people.

He would have to skirt the issue of them going into witness relocation for protection. The very thought of their lives being in danger could make her worry, and he didn't want to give her that kind of stress. He could say it had to do with Betty's recent medical condition. After all, she nearly died! Surely that is something she could understand.

"Okay Ma, the bad news first it is. Miri has had some recent health issues, and currently is in a special facility where she is getting care. To ensure her future health and safety, she'll be needing to be moved elsewhere for an unknown period of time, and I will be joining her."

"So that's why Miri is not here. Oh, that poor girl! You must have been fraught with worry." She went over to him as he put his cup down, and she hugged her son.

He hugged her back tightly. "It was very scary! But what I am most sad about right now, is that I don't know how long we are going to be away, or if we can even come visit."

"Maybe I could come visit you?" She asked hopefully.

"I don't think so Ma. It is not allowed. Everything is secure, and visitors are not allowed. That's what makes me so sad. I finally just got you back, and now we must leave!" Mack had a small tear in his eye as he clung to his mother.

"It is possible that someday we can return, but it is completely unknown when at this point in time."

"How did it come about?" She sat back down in her chair.

"I contacted Woody. You remember my old friend Woody from high school, and college in Baltimore? You probably last saw him at Miri's and my wedding. Well, he's an FBI agent now, and is looking after us. He had the contacts to place us in a special program to make sure Miri gets the best possible care."

Mack handed her Woody's business card. "Here's his card in case of emergency. Please contact him to relay anything to us."

"I do remember Woodrow Everett. He was a very polite boy. He seemed a bit daring at times, as though he liked to see what he could get away with. I kept catching him at the table with the schnapps when you invited him to events at shul. And he incessantly talked about a certain girl that he liked."

"Lily or Lola? Something like that." Mack smiled.

"Your father and I thought he might be a bad influence, but it sounds like he turned out okay." She nodded approvingly.

"Aw, we were just mischievous kids back then." Mack chuckled. "Well, he was maybe more than I was. But really, he's a good guy Ma. He now works to put criminals behind bars. It's a noble and sometimes dangerous profession."

"Indeed." She sighed and said, "Alright. I'm going to think in my mind that you will get to visit. Then if you can, I'll be pleasantly surprised. Now. Please tell me the good news."

"This gives me the greatest of pleasure to tell you." Mack was beaming and took her hands in his.

"You are going to be a Bubby, Ma! Miri is having twins!"

She gave him a huge hug and kissed his cheek. "Mazal Tov, Mack! I am so pleased. I know it has been a long time in coming. And twins! That is such good news. I really do hope you will be able to visit." She put her hands on either side of his cheeks. "I am so proud of you Maccabee."

Mack and his mother continued to talk until he finally had to catch his flight for home. They hugged each other tightly and kissed each other's cheeks, not knowing if they would ever get to see each other again.

Chapter 17
It's Hard to Say Goodbye

Once Mack got back in town, he notified the Albany Family Law Office that he had to resign unexpectedly but could possibly come back in the future. He hadn't gotten many cases there anyway, so it didn't really matter very much. Since he wasn't on a payroll schedule, they said he could come back any time if he needed to. That was a relief.

The last piece of the puzzle in Albany would be arranging to cancel his lease, then somehow move and leave the apartment.

Mack would still have to contact a rabbi in their new community wherever it would be, which was one of the most important items on the agenda. He would be their main contact and the way to blend into the Orthodox community seamlessly.

He knew he'd have to word things carefully concerning Betty and was not at all looking forward to what he thought was sure to be a confrontational subject. He just could not think of her as a machine, but he knew that would be an issue.

Betty was arranging to have a farewell get-together party somehow with the Grady and Kerring families at Caring Corp. It would be very bittersweet.

She contacted Meg and Tom, saying they had to leave and go somewhere unknown. She asked if they'd like to come to their farewell get-together. Of course, they said they would be there, and the Kerrings would be there already.

"*Meg,*" Betty asked, "*do your parents know that I'm still alive? I wouldn't want to exclude them if they did, but the less people who know about this, the better.*"

"I told them, eventually Betty. Daddy loves you, and he was very happy to know that you were okay. I'm sorry, I guess I shouldn't have." Meg tended to be a bit emotional at times, especially now that she was expecting.

"*It's okay Meg, just as long as he or your mom haven't told anyone.*" Betty added, "*Have they?*"

"No, I'm certain of it. When I was kidnapped by Melissa and that other guy, Daddy was very leery to let anyone know anything. But you were able to save me. When you weren't so lucky, and we didn't even know if you were going to make it or not, Daddy made sure to swear Momma to secrecy. She is quiet anyway, but still. He understood that you could possibly be in danger. He was the one who told me that I shouldn't tell anyone. Well, aside from Tom that is."

"*Whew!*" Betty made a sighing sound. "*Indeed. If word ever got out to Gio, I would never be safe. Mack is banking on the fact that the Orthodox community is so closely-knit, and that many people there don't care to have much to do with the secular world except for travel, shopping, and medical visits. They stay mostly within their community area. It seems like the only safe place besides here.*"

"I will miss you so much Betty! You are my best friend, and I thought for sure our children would get to grow up together." Meg started crying and sniffling.

"Meg, I'm not gone yet! And we'll still get to spend time together at the party. Please don't cry, you'll make me start to cry too." Betty muted the connection to let out a small whimper.

"Oh. You are going to invite Kelly, right?" Meg asked.

"I am. I'd really like to invite Mack's old friend Woody. He's the FBI agent in charge of helping us. He may be able to answer a lot of questions about what we can and can't do. I have so many questions and I'm sure you Tom, and Mack do as well. I should contact Mack to ask if we can invite Woody. Okay, I better get going. I'll talk to you later Meg. I love you, my friend," Betty added, trying not to whimper.

"I love you too Betty." Meg sniffed, choking back her tears. "I don't know what I am going to do without you."

"Tom will protect you and your baby. I know it. He's a good man. Bye bye."

Betty called up Mack: *"Michael!"*

"Miriam! What is going on my love?" Mack was still trying hard to get "programmed" himself.

"Can I contact Woody and invite him to our farewell party? I have a lot of questions. So does Meg, and other people too, I'm sure. We all need answers to know how to deal with our 'exit plan.'" Betty wanted to know more.

"I'm sure we could arrange that. It is important that we all know exactly what we are doing for yours, and our family's safety's sake. I think that's an excellent idea. Would you like me to contact him?" Mack offered. He had questions too.

"Sure, Michael, that would be great. Please invite him for next week to our final farewell get-together party for family and friends. Are you coming home soon?" Betty wondered.

"Yes, Miriam, I'm on the way now. I just dropped the keys off at the Albany Family Law Office. They said I could come back any time I wanted." Mack exhaled air through his lips. "Psheww, that was a relief. Last will be the apartment."

"That's wonderful news, Michael. I'll see you in a bit then." Betty disconnected.

Betty went out to look for Robert and Kelly. She found them next to each other in Robert's lab room observing some scientific project they were working closely together on.

"Uhem? Wow, Kelly you really weren't joking!" Betty laughed. "Robbie?" Betty trilled her voice and gave him a smirk, looking at him out of the corners of her eyes.

"Alright Sis, you caught us. And you and Mack were never alone working together, maybe having a little cuddle? Oh, I guess not. It's not allowed. Never mind." He realized.

"Okay, that aside, I'm here to invite you both to our farewell get together party next week. After that, we'll be leaving for good, to who knows where." Betty looked down and kind of shuffled her feet with her hands behind her back, thinking of all the good times she had with Robert.

She then looked up and said, "But, I see, I am leaving you in very good hands. Quite literally!" Then she laughed and ran off down the corridor to find his father.

Kelly giggled. "Robbie, she is such a sister!"

After Betty left, Kelly asked Robert, "What exactly goes through that computer brain of hers? Does she think we were doing something inappropriate? I was raised Catholic and am saving myself for marriage. I don't do things like . . . that!" she said shyly but with pride.

"You must realize that Betty does not even think like that. Dad sheltered the models, and Betty is very childlike in that respect. She only knows about the 'facts of life' strictly from a scientific and medical standpoint, but not so much emotionally. I kind of feel sorry for Mack in that respect." Robert looked down.

"I mean, really, she personally has no physical frame of reference at all. Literally, she was not built with . . . you know . . ." He kind of gestured curves, then just up and down, then he stammered and started to blush in embarrassment.

"I can fix part of that visually anyway," Kelly remarked. "Stay here Robbie, I need to ask her something." Feeling sorry for her, Kelly ran after her. "Betty! Come here a minute!"

Kelly asked Betty woman to woman, did she want to be

more authentic for her babies at least, and she answered yes.

"In that case, follow me!" Kelly took Betty to her lab, where there was a variety of cell-cultured internal organs for implants, and external body parts for post operative surgery.

Kelly had Betty wait in a private room and returned with a pair of newly-grown external prosthetic implants. "Special delivery from the Skin Division! Studies have shown that non-nutritive pacifiers are very beneficial to babies. Now, keep them dry for two days as they bond to your skin," she instructed.

She applied the additions with cellular bonding paste and bandaged her up. Betty was so grateful to better care for the babies. She gently gave Kelly a hug then went on her way.

Dr. Kerring was looking over some new prosthetic hand prototypes in his office. Betty popped her head in the door to see if he was in there, and then she entered the room.

"Dad? You're working late tonight."

"Hi Sweetie! How are you doing? Pretty much back to your old self I see, running around the building. And starting to show a bit I see." He smiled at her affectionately. "I was so looking forward to being a grandfather."

Betty came over to him, put her arms around him and hugged him, resting her head on his shoulder, "And you'll still be a wonderful one, Dad! It looks like the way things are progressing, you may just be a real one. I see Robbie is getting very chummy with Kelly."

"Kelly?" Dr. Kerring seemed surprised.

"The new Skin Division geneticist, Dr. Kelly Carvey?"

"Oh right, Dr. Carvey. I did see them talking together on occasion. I always seem to be the last to know these things."

"Don't worry, I've been watching them and reading them." she giggled. "Really, they are very much alike. I am so happy for Robbie. I was beginning to think he would never find anyone. He is so shy around women, and always has his nose in his work. It looks like Kelly is the same way."

"Did you come here to seek my approval on Kelly? I'm okay with it. But I fear, your dear old dad here just embarrasses Robert, and gets in his way." He continued examining and sometimes waving the hand samples as he spoke.

"Aww? Don't think like that. Robbie loves you; he idolizes you. I think it is natural that he gets a bit self-conscious when he's around a new girlfriend. It's human nature to want to impress her, and he wants to look good. I was that way with Mack even. Don't take it personally."

Then she giggled and added, "I try to tease him every chance I get, in a fun sisterly way of course. Kelly gets my sense of humor. She says she has a lot of siblings. Really, she's very easygoing. A perfect match for Robbie. I couldn't have done better if I tried." Betty smiled thoughtfully.

"So, Dad. I wanted to invite you to our farewell get together. Next week? Then we'll be leaving, and we still don't know where." She looked down and whimpered a little bit.

"Oh Sweetie." He put his arms around her and hugged her and they both started weeping together; Dr. Kerring crying real tears, and Betty whimpering, as they both thought about the possibility that once she and Mack left, they may not ever see each other again.

"I'm so sorry you had to go through so much trauma, Sweetie. It makes me wonder sometimes, were you better off before you were enhanced and acquired real emotions?"

"Quite the contrary Dad. Before then, I don't think I was really, living. I now see and understand that real emotions are what makes a person truly alive, and I am happy to be in that category of personhood. Merely simulated emotions aren't quite the same thing, and certainly not to the same degree anyway. True, I may have experienced a lot of trauma, but look how much I've gained! I have a husband who loves me, and these precious little ones inside of me."

"Robert and I will be there." He nodded emphatically, wiping away residual tears and sniffling.

"Kelly will be there too. I asked her and Robbie already. See you later Dad." Betty left to go to her dorm room.

Mack had just gotten there and was eating a very late dinner before they went to sleep.

"Michael, you must be exhausted! What a day you had wrapping up so many things."

"I am Miriam. I must admit, the closer it gets to the time to leave, the more nervous I get." He sighed deeply.

"What's bothering you? I see something is weighing heavily on your mind and you appear tense," Betty confided.

Mack smiled. "Nope, there is no keeping anything from you! Yes, I'm very worried. I know that the rabbis are just going to view you as a machine. I somehow need to explain to them that you are different. I really don't know how I'm going to convince them. I am around you so much, that I totally forget about your man-made status. It doesn't bother me, you know that. But to most people, they think it is weird. In their eyes, I may as well be married to my autonomous robocar. All because your brain is not organic. They don't believe that you can truly have emotions."

He sighed. "I wish I could just hug you. Technically you are my wife, but not in the eyes of the rabbis. I would like to be able to tell them that even after all this time, I have not even touched you. And," he took a deep breath and sighed, "it's certainly not that I haven't wanted to!" Mack looked her straight in the eyes, gripping the edges of the table tightly.

Betty's processors started tickling with delight again.

"I am hoping they'll give me some kind of leniency, but if I don't follow what they say, it makes me look like I'm sinful, and I will lose total respect in their eyes."

"You're really worried about it, aren't you?" she asked.

He nodded yes, with a sad and concerned look on his face.

"Mack, you know when I was underwater, how I literally saw my life flashing before my eyes? I thought surely I was dying! I saw some strange visions, which at first I thought I was hallucinating. But the more I saw of it, the more I am convinced that it must have been Miri's life. I hadn't told you this yet, but I saw you giving me the cutest little daisy pendant on a necklace in a small, closed room after your marriage ceremony." Betty stared ahead frowning as she thought.

"I did, I gave a daisy necklace to Miri on our wedding day! I had forgotten all about it. The clasp caught on the lace of her wedding dress, then it broke right after that. It fell off and was lost. We never did find it." That is something only Miri could have possibly known." Mack looked into her eyes. "And what Robert said about the DNA code. You really are Miri somehow, aren't you? I've got to explain it all to the rabbis. I just know that it has got to be Hashgacha Pratit, there's no other explanation!"

"Don't worry. I think there are more of these things in my mind somewhere, somehow. As I was under the water, I heard a voice too, saying, 'Tell the rabbi everything. Talk to all three, they will know what to do.' I have no idea what that meant. It was like my subconscious talking to me. And I didn't even know I had one!" Betty was confused, thinking she had hallucinated.

Mack did have some idea what it all might mean, but only time would tell if he was correct. He worried a bit less after that.

Chapter 18
Question and Answer Time

Mack remembered that only a few nights before, just after he came back home from Des Moines, he had seen Meg and Kelly surrounding a very green-haired Betty.

"I just noticed. Your hair is nearly back to its normal color. You must have washed it like crazy!" Mack surveyed her head closely, all over.

"Actually, I did wash it quite a few times, but you know how my semi-organic living skin repairs itself in about one to two days? Apparently, and Kelly confirmed it with Dr. Kerring, the hair follicles and surrounding skin perceived the hair dye as a highly toxic irritant, so it was treated much like it was an injury. That created the perfect conditions for it to try to remodel, going to work to 'heal' itself, and it regenerated faster than usual! At least that is how they explained it to me." Betty thought it was logical. "The hair growth was so fast, that I just trimmed off the excess old green stuff, and voila!"

"I guess that makes sense," Mack agreed.

"Although the green is still there ever so slightly," Betty parted her hair with her fingers exposing her scalp, "it should be pretty much so gone by tomorrow morning. It has been over two days now, and even my incisions for the ectogenesis pod operation healed in that amount of time."

Mack said, "That's a relief. One less thing to explain to the rabbis. The green hair could have served as another reminder that you were not born. If you didn't possess normal colored hair, it makes you look even more synthetic."

"But don't worry, I will still cover my hair when we get to our final destination." Betty smiled at Mack, who now had a little stubbly bit of beard growing in, per her request.

It was time for the farewell party later that night, and Betty put in a larger order from the recently opened kosher Chinese restaurant, this time to be delivered to Caring Corp. She again placed the order in her mind: "*. . . Please include ten fortune cookies and nine pairs of chopsticks. Thanks again, goodbye.*"

Betty went to the employee cafeteria area, and scooted two tables together, covering them with a pretty tablecloth.

Meg and Tom Grady arrived with Jasper and Becky Coates.

Meg said to Betty, "I have a going away present for you. I made one for me too." She handed a nicely wrapped gift to Betty.

"Aw, thank you Meg, you're so sweet!" Betty hugged her.

Kelly and Robert came running in from somewhere within the building, hand in hand, and then Dr. Kerring came in with Mack. The only person missing was the most important guest of all: Woody, who could answer all their questions.

Everyone waited, and then the food arrived. Betty hoped it would be fresh and hot for them. But where was Woody?

"No, no, no!" Mack was concerned about Woody's

absence. He called Woody, and it only turned out he was stuck in traffic but was on the way. "Whew!" Mack sighed.

Woody finally arrived, apologized for being so late, and took his seat. Some people said blessings or grace before their meals as Dr. Kerring audibly sighed, frowned, and looked at his watch. Then everyone dug in. It started out rather quietly; nobody knew quite what to say. They all would miss Betty and Mack. Finally, Betty broke the ice, wanting to learn more about their future.

"We have some questions that I hope you can answer for us, Woody. I don't want to inundate you, but they are pretty important. We need to know exactly what we can and can't do."

"I'll do the best I can to answer," Woody replied, as he used his chopsticks with total precision to eat his food.

"Can you tell us more about the witness protection program?" Mack asked. "It's called WITSEC right?"

Woody responded, "That's the 'US Marshals Witness Security Program' within the Department of Justice under the US Attorney General. It's generally more geared to people who had worked in the mafia or other criminal organizations and are in need of protection for when they testify against their old crime bosses or other members. Usually, the FBI works with former criminals in WITSEC. There's also the Emergency Witness Assistance Program, but it is temporary and limited to thirty days only."

"Oh dear." Betty sounded worried. "Where do we fit in?"

"I need to talk to you two in private about it after everyone else leaves, but I can answer other questions," Woody said.

Meg raised her hand, "Can they still contact us?"

"Well, it is usually done through a third party, you would have a mediator of some kind. Communication cannot be direct. And you can't visit each other; it may not be safe."

"Can we ever leave and go back to our old life?" Betty asked.

"Now, with just about any of these programs, a person and or their family, can decide to leave any time they want to. However, they will no longer be protected."

"What about Mack and Betty's names and identities? And where are they going to live?" Dr. Kerring asked.

Woody was expert in giving instructions. "That is confidential, and only to be known by them. Very important! None of you are to talk to anyone about their existence. As far as anyone outside of this room knows, they are either dead," he pointed at Betty, "or missing," then pointed at Mack.

"Now, when the babies come, they will have their own lives, and everything should be normal to them. Don't go freaking them out by telling them any of this, they don't need to know. They shouldn't be made to feel like they're in danger or have to look over their shoulder. They should be taught the basics of course, don't talk to strangers and those kinds of things, but you want the kids to grow up normal and healthy, not paranoid messes." Woody appeared to have been through this before.

"How should I get in touch with you now?" Mack asked Woody, "Can I use my old phone?"

"No, that's another thing I'll give you later. In between, you'll have to call me on a special burner phone. Once you've relocated, you'll get a permanent one," Woody instructed.

"But because Betty uses her head, there's no replacing that!" Woody raised his eyebrows and smiled.

"My VoIP is private, unlisted, not available to anyone, plus I 'star-6-7' anyone new before I call," Betty added.

"Why can't we call Betty if she is unlisted?" Meg asked.

"If anyone somehow intercepts a communication or traces your call, they'll know she's alive, and it's dangerous for her!"

Robert chimed in, "If and when Marino gets caught, will you put him away for good on the kidnapping charges? Then Betty and Mack can go free, and back to their old lives?"

"It's not so simple," Woody explained. "First of all, they are not being held prisoners! Second, Marino can't be touched on the kidnapping charge. He can maybe be charged with conspiracy, but as usual, from what Betty said, he didn't do it himself, his guys did it. For it to be considered a federal crime, they also would have had to transport her across state lines. Then it could become a case for the FBI."

Meg raised her hand, "I was kidnapped too, but they didn't get away with it, thanks to Betty here!" She smiled at Betty. "Is Melissa and the other guy not going to be in jail very long? Can they kidnap me again? Am I in danger?"

"You shouldn't have to worry; she's going away for a very long time. It was only attempted kidnapping, but she is looking at twenty years maybe? She was also charged with grand theft auto, which may be another five. We suspect Marino gave her the car to use, but he denies it and says she stole it. Now the guy who was with her was never caught, and you didn't get a good look at him, right?" Woody asked.

Meg answered, "No, I never even saw him. He stuck a bag over my head from behind."

Meg then started crying. "They forced me at gunpoint to tell them what happened to their money, and I said that Betty was the one who intervened with the authorities to recover Daddy's stolen money. I'm so sorry Betty! I think it was all my fault that you got kidnapped!" She cried even harder.

Betty ran over to her and put her arms around her to comfort her best friend, "It wasn't your fault, Meg. You had to protect yourself and your baby. It's okay, I forgive you."

Woody wanted clarification, "But you knew this lady Melissa who took you?" Meg nodded yes, as she sniffled.

Woody pointed out, "If she was working for Marino and she botched the job, she's probably in far more danger herself than you are, even in jail. I think you're safe, because the other guy could not be identified. Just stay aware of your surroundings and any strangers, and you should be okay."

"That was the whole reason Marino wanted to get rid of Betty when the ransom wasn't dropped. He knew she could identify all of them. She had to go." He did a cutthroat gesture.

"Can this Marino guy be put away at all? Will Betty and Mack ever be safe?" Tom asked.

"What Betty provided us with is information that will hopefully lead to charges against him personally. I can't really talk about the case, but with the help of her proof, we may be able to get him. It still can possibly take a few years."

"Years!" . . . "Years?" Woody's audience repeated sadly.

"Quite possibly. It's serious business everyone. It isn't just a matter of happily getting to move to a nice new place and starting over. There is a cost of leaving behind one's old life, family, and friends, and maybe never being able to return. That is why the bureau is willing to pay for the huge sacrifice that a person, or a person along with their family, must make."

Kelly asked, "Can we email? What about chat groups? Is there any way to contact them besides an intermediary?"

"No, I'm sorry, there isn't," Woody reiterated.

"What about when the babies come?" Betty had a very important question. "I need to go to Caring Corp. to deliver when it is time. Nobody else knows how to do the procedure for removal of the ectogenesis pod and delivery of the babies other than the Kerrings. It is a major surgery for me. How will that work if I can't come back here to see them again?"

Woody thought long and hard before answering this one.

"Since it is such a special circumstance, we will have to work something out. Obviously, the life of your children is of primary importance. The fact that they need special care, should be ample reason to comply with that request. Perhaps we can have a special ambulance on standby as the time approaches. Can you tell exactly when they will come? Is it like for a regular human woman with contractions and labor and all that kind of stuff, or do they just suddenly pop out?"

Betty laughed. "They don't just pop out, it's a specific operation. My fetal activity monitor should give me warning by, maybe, up to a day before?" Betty questioned Dr. Kerring.

"Yes, most likely," Dr. Kerring confirmed. "The G-3s have the same monitoring equipment that you do. It should pick up on and alert you to an increase of fetal activity within the pod. Your touch sensitivity might even pick up their movement as well if they start kicking hard enough."

Robert added, "You, or whoever the intermediary is, should let us know as soon as this happens. Could we maybe get alerted with an emergency call or something? We really need to be well prepared ahead of time since Betty is not already on-site like the G-3s are automatically."

"I'll see what I can work out with the bureau. Human lives are at stake, so yes, they will definitely take that into consideration," Woody replied seriously.

Chapter 19

The Farewell Party Ends

All the main food had been eaten, and all the questions anyone could think of had been asked. It was a different mood than that of Betty's personhood victory party. Nobody wanted to go home, they all wished they could just remain there with Betty and Mack.

"Okay everyone, let's read our fortunes now!" Betty broke open a cookie, mustering up as cheery of an attitude as she could. "Who wants my cookie?" Betty waved it in the air.

"I'll take it, Meg replied. "I'm still hungry!"

"Well, you are eating for two." Tom smiled sweetly at her.

"Yeah, Betty, how do you not ever get hungry?" Meg asked. "You have two buns in the oven." Everyone laughed.

"Well, for one thing, I have no stomach! I don't have the foggiest idea what hunger would even feel like." Betty looked down a bit puzzled, cocking her head.

Dr. Kerring opened his cookie and had trouble getting his fortune out. He unrolled the slip of paper to reveal his.

"'You simply haven't lived until you've learned to let go.' Hmm." He stroked his stubbly beard, letting it sink in.

"There goes Dad getting the logical ones again. But I think I know what it means, Dad." Robert looked a bit serious. "It's April and Mom. You need to go on with your life. Maybe look for another life partner. Hey, look at me. I just found someone special." He smiled at Kelly and gently tapped her on the nose. She smiled back shyly and giggled.

Dr. Kerring got a tear in his eye. "You're probably right Robert. It is just very hard to let go. I still miss them."

"Oh Robbie, why'd you have to go and dampen the mood?" Betty said. "Dad's going to go into 'Crybaby Kerring' mode."

"Why must I keep getting called that?" he snapped. "Thanks a lot, Jasp for letting everyone in on that one." He rolled his eyes and frowned. "I'll never live it down now."

"Alright Dad, I'm sorry I said that. But just when was the last time you cried?" Betty asked.

"Let's see, last week? No. You're right it was just a couple days ago, when we were together, and you invited me here."

"See? But it's not at all a bad thing to be emotional, Dad. Aren't I proof of that?" Betty said proudly.

"Then again, you didn't have any problems until you got your emotions Sis," Robert pointed out.

Betty jokingly frowned at Robert and explained herself.

"I had nothing when I had no emotions. That is my whole point! When you have feelings, it proves you are alive. You just need to learn how to deal with them in a positive way. Keep on being emotional Dad. Crying or not. It is a good trait to have. Always remember that! It's very healthy."

She got up and went over to give him a hug and he rested his head on her shoulder. "I know you miss them," Betty whispered in his ear, and he shook his head emphatically.

"I'll go." Woody hoped to lighten the heavy mood. "'Be slow to respond, not quick to react.' Very important in my line of work, unless of course someone's about to shoot me." He smiled and made a shooting gun sign to his head saying, "Pshhew!"

"Now let's see if I get another 'Star Trek' quote this time." Mack cracked open his fortune cookie. "Nope, this one says, 'Let things unfold. Relinquish control.' That is very profound, especially in our current situation. I guess it means I should have faith that everything will work out for the best."

Tom read his, "'Get lost in the right direction.' As a pilot, is that a good thing or not?" He frowned in thought.

Becky Coates related her fortune, "'You love peace.' Now wait just a minute, that's the same exact one I got the last time! Is someone trying to tell me something? Jasper, Honey. Am I not peaceful enough?"

Jasper responded, "Dear, you are probably the most peaceful person I know!"

"Yeah Momma, Daddy's right," Meg added.

"Maybe I'm just boring," Becky said sadly.

"Naw Becky. Being quiet and peaceful isn't boring, it's being stable and reliable. That is what I love about you, Dear!" Jasper leaned over toward her to give her a kiss.

"Aww," Meg responded. "I hope Tom and I will be just like you two when we get older."

"Now I'm old?" Becky raised her eyebrows looking plaintively at Jasper, and he sighed.

"Not to me, Honey. You will always be as pretty and young as the day I first met you." Then the whole table of people said, "Awwww", at the same time and laughed.

Meg frowned. "Mine is the opposite of yours Momma. 'Flow with things rather than insist they flow with you.' But don't I do that? Gee, they were so accurate the last time!"

Kelly opened hers and stated, "'Learn from everyone.' That is very true. Everyone has something to teach.'"

Robert read his fortune, "'Everything that is, was first a dream.' That sounds just like Caring Corporation. Right Dad?" he said cheerily with a smile.

Betty was satisfied with hers and waited till last. "Okay, here is my fortune, it is a good one too. 'Wake up believing today will be better than yesterday.' Yes, I do that all the time."

"With that in mind, let's all make a toast." Woody raised his glass. "Here's to a new life for Betty and Mack!"

Everyone clinked their glasses together and agreed.

"We love you guys," Meg added.

"Another new life that is, "Mack said. "We barely got to start out with the first new life together."

"Sometimes, I feel like a cat, having nine lives!" Betty

remarked. "I think I've had more new lives than any of you!"

Kelly laughed remarking, "And your code, and Miri's and the babies' DNA do have C-A-T in the string a couple of times."

All faces turned toward Kelly as she put her hand to her mouth. "Was I not supposed to tell anyone?"

Everyone started looking at each other, wondering what the meaning of it all was, but it sounded very impressive.

"Robert?" Dr. Kerring said sternly, "Did you start looking into Betty's coding again when I told you not to?"

"No, he didn't Dr. Kerring," Kelly came to Robert's defense immediately. "He told me specifically that he was not allowed to. He had merely been checking out the babies' welfare. He had their DNA sample and thought it looked very similar to what he saw of Betty's coding that he had recorded on his paper. He asked for my help to investigate. Robbie could have looked into it further, but he didn't."

Jasper, Becky, Meg, Tom and Woody all looked confused.

"What does it mean? Can someone please explain it to those of us who don't have a medical background?" Jasper asked.

Mack decided to tell their close friends their findings.

"I'll try to simplify it. One day Robert inspected Betty's coding to see what made her unique. Normally impossible, besides the 1s and 0s, he saw letters; all of which corresponded to the four letters in a string of DNA. He compared it to my late wife Miri's DNA, and it was a perfect match. And of course, half of it matched the babies' DNA signatures, or string rather. I say it's a miracle, but it appears that Betty here, not only has the face of my late wife, but also has her DNA somehow built into her coding."

"So, Betty is really Miri?" Meg asked.

"It would seem so," Kelly answered.

"This must not leave this room. If anyone got wind of it, perhaps the regulatory committees would want to dissect all our models, looking to see if there were others like her. We know there are not, but still!" Dr. Kerring looked worried.

"Nobody in this room can speak of it anyway. If it's known that Betty's alive, she'd be in danger," Woody reminded them.

"Does it mean that Betty is really human?" Meg said wide-eyed and smiling.

"No, it just means, that we can't explain it. Maybe she has Miri's soul though," Kelly commented hopefully.

"Oh, come on!" Dr. Kerring crossed his arms frowning.

"Dad? Can you honestly say that you don't think Mom and April could be happily looking down at us from some other plane of existence?" Robert defended Kelly now, as his father looked at him in total disbelief.

"Do you really think, that when you die, it's over, and there is nothing else? I may have agreed with you for many years, because I too was mad that Mom and April were taken from us. But Betty has actually opened my eyes to some new possibilities. I still may not know exactly what to believe about the grand scheme of things. But you are a doctor and a scientist, and you observe the miracles of life! How can you just take what we do here every day at Caring Corp. for granted? I will get off my soapbox now, but I know that there are others at this table, including Betty there who is man-made, and they believe that there is an ultimate Creator and something else out there. Please, Dad, have some respect for them."

Dr. Kerring sat there quietly, frowning, and staring into space, stroking his beard. He was speechless. Robert had never confronted him like that before in his life.

"Well? This party just keeps getting better and better," Betty said with slight sarcasm. She looked down sadly.

"I'm sorry everyone, I really meant for this to be a happy, last time get-together. I understand that everyone is a bit on edge and stressed psychologically because we may not see each other for a while after this." She pointed her finger in the air and added, "I will not let myself believe that we will never see each other again. I just can't! But please, for me and Mack. Make our last moments here together happy!"

"I'm sorry, Sis," Robert said. Others apologized as well.

"I am sorry too Sweetie. I'll say nothing more." Dr. Kerring got up from his chair and went over to Betty. He put his arms around her and looked into her pretty brown eyes, trying not to tear up although he did anyway, and said, "You know I love you. I wish you and Mack the best of luck and happiest life possible. If you can, please send pictures of the grandkids." Then he remembered, "Although you have to come back here to deliver them!" That brought a smile to his face.

"There you go Dad. I'll be seeing you soon!" She smiled back.

"Goodbye everyone," Dr. Kerring said to all in the room. "I have work I need to do. Dr. Carvey? Robert?" He nodded at them very formally, as though he didn't even know them.

Robert sighed. "I can't change him, and I hate to say we may not have the happy courtship I had imagined. I'm sorry Kelly," he whispered to her, and she flashed half a smile.

Betty felt bad that Kelly was in the middle of the situation and added, "Dad probably feels he's losing Robbie to you."

Mack said, "Give him time to adjust. I was grieving over Miri, my father, and somewhat of a loss of my mother for many years, and then Betty came along." He smiled.

"She took me totally by surprise. Really, I can relate to your father a bit. I felt anger at first with Miri gone, but also a profoundly deep sadness. Some people may never recover, like my brother Barry. But then others like me, can have a reawakening when someone new comes along. She . . ." Mack smiled, gesturing toward Betty, "totally changed my life. It may be that your father needs the same, to pull him out of himself, and out of despair. I'm hoping that maybe your words made it to his heart somehow. I'd imagine it must be a sad and lonely existence if one is not at all religious." Mack patted Robert on the back.

"Thanks Mack," Robert replied, and Kelly nodded.

"Well, it's getting past our bedtime." Jasper got up and then Becky followed. He went over to Betty and said, "Don't pay attention to Kenny. He just had to blow off some steam. He was always like that." Then he whispered in her ear, "When he wasn't crying that is." Jasper laughed.

"I love my old friend Kenny, but sometimes he takes life way too seriously. Goodbye Betty." He hugged her and went over to Mack. "I will see you guys around. Take care of yourselves." Jasper patted him on the back.

Tom came over to hug Mack and Betty, who were now standing side by side. "I'll miss you guys. You know it won't be the same without you." Betty nodded.

Meg ran over to Betty and burst into tears, "I don't want to leave you!" She hugged Betty tightly and Betty hugged her back, then started whimpering. Mack looked down holding onto the back of his chair, biting his lower lip.

"You have to be strong, for me and for your baby," Betty said. Meg emphatically nodded, wiping her nose with a napkin.

Betty thought of something cheerful. "I never asked you Meg, do you know what your baby is going to be?"

"Oh," she sniffled, "we wanted to be surprised, but I have a feeling it is going to be a girl." Meg rubbed her belly.

Betty looked at Tom, and he replied, "Whatever it will be, we will love them. I wouldn't mind it being a little girl."

They all had one last group hug as was customary, and then Tom and Meg left. Robert and Kelly came over next.

"See you later!" Robert said, and shook Mack's hand, then both he and Kelly hugged Betty as they were going.

"And Kelly?" Betty whispered, as she turned back to look.

"Thank you so much for the going away present. I'll take good care of them!" Betty winked at Kelly. Kelly got a big smile and gave Betty a thumbs up, then she and Robert left.

"What was that all about?" Mack asked Betty.

"Never mind. It doesn't concern you, now," she answered.

"Whew!" Mack looked at Woody. "It didn't go quite as well as expected." He looked down and shook his head.

"Really Michael, all things considered, I think it really did go pretty well," Woody concluded.

"You see, there is this whole psychological aspect to it, where people may feel many emotions all at once, and usually have heightened sensitivity. They're all people you are close to, and it is as if they are losing you forever. It was a nice idea Miriam, but when you get a lot of different people together who are each experiencing grief in their own way, it is bound to be heavy and tense at times. But really, you managed to pull it off!" Woody gave Betty a nod of approval.

She grinned happily.

Chapter 20

Preparing to Move

"Okay, now that we're alone, let's get down to business," Woody announced. "I was getting everything together before I came here, which was partly why I was late." Woody went to get his briefcase. "Here's your new burner phone as promised. I'll take your old one, Michael."

Mack handed his old phone over to Woody.

"Once we get to your new location, I'll give you a permanent phone. Now, I managed to pull some strings," Woody exclaimed proudly.

"The State of New York has its own program, Victim Witness Assistance, and we rely on a few different local government agencies to help provide funding for basic living expenses, a car, medical care, and accommodations. Miriam is considered a 'Fact Witness.' Since she is such a valuable asset to the country, having provided the FBI with video footage and her GPS information, they considered it as good as if she had testified in person at a trial. There are special circumstances, in that you are already thought to be dead by the perpetrators of the crimes, so it all worked out."

"Wow, Woody. You've really been busy! I am so thoroughly impressed. I know how long it can often take to cut through all the bureaucratic red tape!" Mack remarked.

Woody said, "I have something else for you two." He reached inside his briefcase. "Here are your brand-new IDs!"

"Oh, look Michael, it has an address, '1360 East Thirty-Fourth Street.' Is it a real or fake address?" Betty asked. "Or does that mean . . . you already have a place for us?"

"Sure does!" Woody grinned. "There's a house in the East Midwood area of Brooklyn, New York that just became available. It was seized from con artists running a scam that tried to bilk older people out of retirement money, promising they would get this beautiful model home. They never came through with their empty promises. Just took the money and ran."

"Oh no, that's so sad!" Betty exclaimed.

Mack growled, "I really hate it when older people get taken advantage of! I'm so glad you caught them, Woody. It is such a pet peeve of mine."

"The house was originally designated to be an FBI safe house. It was all paid off except for back taxes, so the FBI bought it for about two thousand dollars, and it was in perfect condition. It was reappropriated to be given to a great American hero and her husband." Woody smiled, handing Betty the keys.

"Oh, my goodness Michael, our very own house!" Betty held her hand up to her mouth and started to go hug Woody. She stopped herself, remembering that she couldn't do that anymore where they would be going."

"Good save Miriam!" Mack said, knowing she was a hugger.

"There are schools and several synagogues nearby, all within walking distance." Woody pulled out a community directory from his briefcase and handed it to them.

"This has lists of Jewish establishments in the community, including kosher restaurants and grocery shopping in the area. It also has the histories of the various synagogues, and phone numbers for their rabbis. It's a good start so that you can make an intelligent decision. I know how important it is for you and your situation."

Mack and Betty nodded in agreement.

Woody smiled and continued, "Your house has three bedrooms, one and a half baths, in a very nice neighborhood."

"Do we pay rent on it, or can we eventually buy it? How does it work Woody?" Mack wanted to know their options.

"The bureau has ways of dealing with other government agencies. The FBI had first dibs and paid off all the back taxes owed from the con artists. It always seems to be taxes that gets crooks in trouble." Woody chuckled. "The deed is now in your new names, just as though you bought it from the county at a foreclosure auction. It's already yours free and clear!"

Woody patted Mack on the back. "It had to be this way for your cover to work. Your backstory is that you two are simply moving to a new neighborhood now that you are expecting a family, just like many ordinary people do.”

“And it’s all true!” Betty acknowledged.

“That could have been a real problem, because her programming does not allow her to lie. I can’t thank you enough my old friend!” Mack replied.

“And here are the keys to your new car, Michael. Well, used, but new for you.” He grinned. “We get impounded and seized cars coming in all the time. It may not be quite as nice as your old robocar, but it’s in good working condition, and the title is in your name. All completely paid for.”

“Thank you!” Betty and Mack exclaimed as Woody smiled.

“What do we do about our old belongings?” Betty asked.

“Leave the moving to us. We’ll move your stuff and you too, a few times before reaching the final location,” Woody replied.

Mack looked worried, “I haven’t been to my apartment in a few weeks since I’ve been staying at Caring Corp.”

“Actually, that’s perfect! I told your landlord you’d been missing, and that we were going to remove your personal effects and send them to relatives. And look, I even made up these missing posters with your name and picture on it to complete the illusion. I’m going to have them posted around the neighborhood in the general vicinity of your apartment tomorrow. Hopefully, word on your ‘missing’ status will get back to Marino.”

“Okay Woody. That looks nice. Let’s hope it works.”

Woody held up a finger. “But wait, there’s more! Just

temporarily, so you guys don't look as you normally do. Michael, I know you prefer your yarmulke, but during this transitionary time, maybe wear this baseball cap so you can blend into a crowd, and Miriam can wear this blonde wig."

"Ugh," Mack remarked scratching his chin, "and growing out a beard takes a bit of getting used to. It's so itchy!"

"That's excellent Michael, I noticed," Woody acknowledged. "Miriam, I know how much you love your gold medal, but I'd highly advise keeping it out of sight in a drawer. It's way too risky if anyone sees it and starts asking you questions about it."

The next morning, Woody's crew headed to Mack's apartment, getting ready to start to move their things. There were also other people who came to hang up missing posters.

Mack had his own issues to deal with: getting Betty ready for life in the Orthodox Jewish community where they were headed. Fortunately, she was a quick study and learned at an astounding rate. He quizzed her often on subjects like keeping kosher, and what to do and what not to do on Shabbat, their Sabbath day. The strict laws literally covered every area of life. She had to be able to give intelligent answers to people and understand the reasons behind them.

The biggest challenge would be to get their chosen rabbi to see Betty as a person and not just a machine. Mack asked Woody if it was possible, for the rabbi to call the Kerrings for any technical questions, and that was okay. Dr. Robert Kerring would be able to help with the explanation of the DNA code, or lack thereof, with the help of Dr. Kelly Carvey. Hopefully between all their evidence, they'd be convinced of Betty's genuineness.

Woody and his crew arrived at Caring Corp. very late at night after all the staff had gone home. The only ones around were patients in their beds or rooms, and the caregiver models that watched over them. It was the only way to ensure that Betty and Mack could be transported safely without fear of being followed. No cars or other vehicles were in sight.

"Are you ready Miriam and Michael?" Woody asked them.

Mack took a deep breath and blew out and Betty made a sighing sound, and they both said, "Yes, let's do this."

They entered the large plain van, and Woody's crew loaded up the items they had brought with them to Caring Corp. Betty made sure to bring four extra portable chargers, one of each type for every connection possible. She was determined she would never be without one again.

Betty popped her head out of the back of the van and waved to her G-4 model sisters one last time. They all sent well wishes in their minds to her. She let out a little whimper, remembering how she had left the very first time with Jimmy, as she glanced up at the Caring Corp. logo she had designed. It all seemed like a lifetime ago.

The crew closed the doors of the van, with the loading of their items now complete, and Woody banged twice on the doors to signal them to go. It would have been almost a three-hour drive if they went straight to Brooklyn, but they would transfer temporarily to motels a few times on the way. They would be under protective surveillance the entire time.

The items being moved from their apartment would take an entirely different route and be transferred three different times to other trucks and storage facilities before making it to the final location of their new home. All these procedures ensured that Mack, Betty, and their belongings could not be followed.

Mack had asked if there was kosher food available, and Woody made sure to provide some shelf-stable meals that were self-heating. They were adequate, but not much to write home about. He was just happy to be there with Betty by his side. Nothing else mattered to him now, except for her welfare and the welfare of their future children.

They arrived at the first stop: a nice motel with plainclothes security officers posted outside. Nothing eventful happened, and things were going smoothly. Betty unwrapped Meg's gift. It was a homemade scrapbook full of articles about Betty. She put her medal of honor with it and packed them away.

After two more nights, Betty and Mack finally arrived in Brooklyn, a few miles away from their destination. They overnighted in the very last location: an old motel from the 1960s. Betty noticed a timer box next to the bed she was sitting on. She wondered what it was for and turned the little dial. It started shaking her! She had never felt anything like it before in her life, and she started laughing. She had great fun playing with the Magic Fingers Vibrating Bed. It made her laugh so hard.

"What do people use this for?" She giggled, as she jumped on and off the bed from a sitting position and then rolled around on it. "It tickles my touch sensitivity sensors in the oddest way. Tee-hee-hee! I wonder if the babies can feel it too. Tee-hee-hee-hee! This is so much fun!"

Mack answered, "Well, it can massage a person's back when they are tired and have aching muscles. Probably the movers of our stuff could use one of these about now, especially the ones who had to move our heaviest furniture."

"Aw, why not," Mack said, as he turned on the Magic Fingers dial and playfully jumped onto the other bed to see what all the fuss was about. "You're right, it does kind of tickle!" He giggled along with Betty.

The timers went off and the beds stopped vibrating. Mack had plopped onto his back on the bed, then rolled over to face Betty. They looked at each other, smiling contentedly.

Mack fell asleep totally exhausted from all the stress of that week. Betty went and plugged one of her chargers in, and she went into sleep mode as well. They both got a very good night's rest and charging session that evening.

Tomorrow was going to be a whole new adventure, and Mack was ready to fight for his family.

Chapter 21
A New Battle

Woody called in the morning, letting Mack and Betty know that the moving truck had arrived, and all their items were unloaded and put into place in their new house.

Woody had overseen the packing up of the kitchen so that Mack needn't worry about his kosher items getting mixed up. He had enough to worry about, and Woody didn't want his old friend to have to be stressed about anything else.

Dr. Kerring had coordinated with Woody to send Betty a surprise gift for their new home: a brand-new charging bed that plugged directly into a wall outlet. It was delivered that same day. He knew Betty would come to need it more often throughout the day as the babies grew larger inside of her. She was already starting to get tired more easily and more often than before, as the filtration and nutrient systems ran more frequently, putting an extra strain on her.

Betty was also provided with extra nutrient tanks and waste deposit tanks since she would no longer be at Caring Corp.

Woody's crew were to make their rounds to Caring Corp. once a month to pick up new tanks and return the empty ones. The number of tanks increased each month as the babies grew. It was a slick operation deemed necessary by the bureau since the babies' lives depended on it. It would continue until they were born. Once Betty gave birth, the crew would pick up and deliver cell-cultured human milk to feed the twins. Every aspect of their care was meticulously planned out.

When Betty and Mack arrived at their new home that morning, Woody led Mack to his car in the back and gave him the permanent phone listed in his new name. Mack could now schedule an appointment to meet with a rabbi and tell him emphatically that everything was to be kept confidential since their lives were at stake, which of course was the standard policy of rabbis anyway.

Now that they were finally there, Mack knew he had a very hard task ahead of him. He must try to find a rabbi who would be receptive of their situation. That would be hard when the normal opinion of a man-made humanoid robot is that they don't have a soul and are considered just like a machine.

Just as with her freedom trial, he had to get them to see Betty as a person, but he wasn't sure just how he would do it yet. He remembered his farewell fortune cookie, "Let things unfold, relinquish control," and tried not to worry.

Mack looked carefully through the directory Woody had given to them. There was just something that attracted him to a particular "right-wing" or stricter Modern Orthodox synagogue, which was only a few blocks away from their house. Their Rav, Rabbi Fishel Silverstein did a radio show that aired once a month. He was also a judge in the local Jewish Court. He had a medium sized family of five, still being relatively young. It sounded like a perfect fit!

He called up the synagogue office, and asked to make an appointment with, or to speak with the rabbi. The secretary made an appointment for the next morning, but she invited him to the afternoon service in about a half hour. Mack decided to come. He could at least meet the rabbi then. He went there and felt right at home. Being on the run for a while, he hadn't been able to pray with a group of ten men as was normally required.

Afterward, Rabbi Silverstein came over to greet the new face in the crowd. They shook hands, and Mack introduced himself.

"Hello Rabbi Silverstein, my name is Michael Gold. My wife Miriam and I just moved into the area. You could say we're 'shul-shopping.'"

"Very nice to meet you, Michael." Rabbi Silverstein was very personable and approachable. He was a pleasant man with slight gray streaks mixed in his short, neatly groomed beard.

"We have a relatively young congregation here. Do you have any children? There's a nice play area in the back."

"Right now, we are expecting twins! Our very first children." Mack grinned happily.

"Lovely! It's always so nice to hear of a growing family. I'll have to introduce your wife to mine." The rabbi smiled.

"That would be wonderful, thank you," Mack replied. "I read that you have a radio show. What is it about?"

"Oh yes, once a month." Rabbi Silverstein nodded. "It's basically introducing Jewish topics to those who are newly observant, or those who just want to know more about it. Sometimes people call in with questions who know nothing about Judaism or Orthodoxy. They seem to have a certain fascination about it. Especially to non-Jews who think that all Orthodox Jews are like the Amish."

"I know, really!" Mack chuckled. "Some seem to get us mixed up with a lot of other religions. I tell them, 'Yes, we believe in blood transfusions, even organ donation, and we are pro-technology.'" Mack was also trying to get a sense of this rabbi's perspectives on technology for Betty's sake.

"True, too many people see TV shows depicting all Orthodox Jews as being so rigid and unhappy, wanting to escape their 'prison-like' way of life. I aim to try and change that. I mean sure, there are those sects of Orthodoxy that are completely anti-technology, not wanting to use the internet and smart phones, but not everyone is that way. We live in a modern world, and it can be used for good. I'm sorry

Michael, I tend to talk a lot. I guess that's why they convinced me to go on radio." Rabbi Silverstein laughed.

The rest of the men had left the building to go home, and it was just the rabbi and Mack left there alone.

"I had set up an appointment with the secretary to talk to you tomorrow morning after services," Mack added.

"Oh, very nice. Did you want to bring your wife?"

"I may just do that. Thank you, Rabbi Silverstein. We do have some very personal things to discuss with the Rav." Mack referred to him in third person, as it was a manner of showing respect. Many big rabbis expected it.

"Oh, don't worry about addressing me that way. We're very down to earth and casual here. I am no different or better than anyone else," Rabbi Silverstein replied.

"Okay, Rabbi Silverstein. Should my wife come later?"

"It's up to her. The women's section enters from over there." He pointed to a wall with a curtain across it. "Most women don't come in the morning on weekdays, but she's more than welcome to if she likes. There are plenty of prayer books. Or if she's busy, she can come after services at about 7:30 a.m. My office is down the hallway from the social hall to the left. Later tomorrow morning, my wife will probably be there with some of the younger children. They're starting to prepare some of the food for a wedding on Sunday."

"Thank you, Rabbi. It has been such a pleasure to meet

you!" Mack shook his hand again. "I will see you tomorrow morning. Bye."

Mack returned to their new home to find Betty organizing. She had already fixed Mack's dinner. Things were looking up!

"Hello Miriam, how are things going so far?" Mack smiled at her sweetly.

"Hi Michael. Things are coming along, I organized two of the bedrooms, but I thought you might want to use one for an office, so I left it alone. It's kind of a storage room for now," she replied.

"How do you do so much, my love? Oh, you go into your hyper mode where your processors speed up and you go super-fast?" Mack asked.

"How did you guess?" Betty looked surprised.

"I suppose I've lived with you long enough to know." He chuckled. "I made an appointment for tomorrow morning after Shacharit to talk to the rabbi," Mack informed her.

"'Shacharit.' Hebrew; Definition: The Jewish morning prayer service," Betty said aloud as she looked it up.

"You're probably going to be doing that a lot around here. Often, English is interlaced with Hebrew or sometimes even Yiddish words. But you might want to just think it as you look it up instead of audibly saying it," Mack cautioned.

"Understood." Betty nodded and smiled.

"Did you want to come tomorrow?" Mack asked.

"If you think I should," Betty said uneasily.

"You can come for prayers, or come later, it's up to you. He showed me where the women's section was. You can read Hebrew, right?" He smirked, knowing fully well that she could.

"Yes Dear, I just need to remember to switch it from left to right to right to left. I am naturally programmed for LTR, so it takes a bit of getting used to switching to RTL mode. Yes, I can go for prayers. I can interpret and analyze as I go. I can even scan it into my memory banks."

"Don't scan it, it is frowned upon to memorize them and say prayers by rote. It should be a new, fresh reading each time," Mack instructed. 'That's how you mean it as you say it."

"Okay, no scanning. I'll remember that for future times. Your dinner is ready if you want to eat now, Michael. It's in the oven keeping warm."

"Thank you, Miriam. As always, taking good care of me."

Mack sat down to eat, and Betty sat down opposite him.

"It is very important to have a good rapport with one's rabbi and to feel comfortable talking to him. So far, Rabbi Silverstein appears to be very nice, and so easy to talk to. He seems to embrace technology, but we shall see."

Morning came and they both got ready to go. Betty had her blonde wig on, and appropriate dress: a buttoned-up shirt with three-quarter length sleeves, and a skirt below the knees.

"I'm so nervous," Betty said. "I have never met a rabbi before, at least that I know of. How do I look?"

"You look gorgeous as always." Mack smiled at her.

When they arrived, Mack showed her to the entrance of the women's section, then he went into the men's section.

Betty took a prayer book and switched her reading mode to RTL. The service started. Betty wished she could be there with Mack, but she knew she shouldn't peek through the curtain. She understood that the reason for it was so the men would concentrate fully on their prayers without the distraction of pretty women.

She periodically switched to infrared vision to watch Mack. She was intrigued by how the men moved back and forth as they prayed, a motion they called "shuckling". It was a bit contagious, and she even found herself doing it after a while. She finished reading her prayers in five minutes. Meanwhile, the men took about thirty.

Perhaps I should not have done my speed-reading like I usually do. But it isn't that I don't mean what I'm saying, Betty thought to herself.

She switched back to LTR mode so she could read English again. It would be very embarrassing if she had neglected to do that and were to read everything backwards.

Chapter 22
What to Do?

The service finished. Mack came to the women's section door to motion Betty over. They went down to the rabbi's office, where he cheerfully greeted them and offered Betty an extra seat.

"So, Michael. How do you like it here so far?"

"It's very nice! You have a beautiful building here. This is my wife, Miriam, Miriam Elizabeth." Mack pointed toward Betty with his hand. "This is Rabbi Fishel Silverstein."

"Nice to meet you Rabbi Silverstein," she said with a nod.

"It's a pleasure to meet you Miriam," Rabbi Silverstein said with a smile. He got a thoughtful look, as if he were trying to place where he had seen her before, then shook his head.

"Michael, you said you had something very personal to discuss. Of what nature, may I ask?" He looked concerned.

"We need to speak to you in total confidence."

"Of course! Whatever it is will never leave this room."

"Rabbi," Mack started whispering and leaned in toward him, "we are in a witness protection program, and nobody can learn of our true identities. That is the first thing. Now, Michael ben Moshe is my Hebrew name, and Michael is now my legal name. Miriam here, technically does not have a Hebrew name, although she would be Miriam Elisheva."

"Miriam Elisheva," the rabbi repeated slowly, again in

deep thought. Betty noticed that he smiled ever so slightly.

"Oh my, how am I going to tell this over?" Mack buried his head in his hands and shook his head.

"Take your time Michael, it's okay. I can imagine you've probably been through a lot. I can cancel or postpone my later appointments if need be. It looks like what you have to say is very hard for you, and important," Rabbi Silverstein noted.

Mack breathed in a deep sigh. "It has been hard, and sometimes confusing to know what exactly to do. I just want to do the right thing, Rav." Mack looked him in the eyes.

Betty felt a bit uneasy. Then suddenly, she felt a little flutter and scanned the ectogenesis pod. She saw the babies shifting themselves slightly. "Oh!" she commented.

"What's wrong, are the babies okay?" Mack looked at her a bit worried. She didn't usually remark about things.

"They just shifted, Michael. I'm okay, sorry to interrupt."

"Do you watch the news at all, Rabbi Silverstein?"

"I try to keep up with current events, and what is going on in government, why?" the rabbi asked with a puzzled look.

"My wife is a national hero, or was, but she was kidnapped and is a witness. She nearly died trying to save our children, and that is why we had to be relocated. It was very much in the news. She's believed to be dead by her kidnappers."

Mack sighed. "I love my wife with all my heart. But she is not really an Orthodox Jew. I think she would like to be, am I right?" He looked at Betty questioningly, and she nodded yes, very emphatically with a big hopeful smile and sparkling eyes.

"Oh, so you want to convert. That's not a problem. Converts are very welcome here. Have you had any formal training?"

Mack replied, "Somewhat, but she has the entire 'Talmud' and all of 'Tanach' memorized, as well as many other books. I taught her most everything she needs to know."

"Wow, that is impressive! I don't have the 'Talmud' memorized. Which one, Yerushalmi or Bavli?" he asked.

"Both," Betty answered.

Rabbi Silverstein proceeded to quiz her on the spot about all the various tractates on many subjects. Betty aced every answer.

"Whew! I wish some of my students were so well-versed. Michael, your wife is amazing!" the rabbi exclaimed. "She should have no problems with conversion, I am surprised she hasn't converted before now! I can arrange to get three rabbis together."

"But there is yet another problem," Mack added, "which you may just take issue with; and my last rabbi did."

"What could possibly be the problem?" The rabbi chuckled.

"She was not born human. You could say she has a prosthetic brain. She was made by a man. She literally had to go to court to win her freedom and official personhood, because she was a slave, and a badly abused one at that! I married her civilly to help her be free, and for her safety she has lived with me ever since. Now, I know that civil marriage has no relevance in the Jewish world. But she has emotions! She has saved many human lives, and now she is carrying my children," Mack just blurted everything out.

"And I have his late wife's face and name," Betty added.

"Wow! It's a lot to process!" The rabbi agreed, then frowned and tugged at his beard. "I remember it now," he mumbled.

"I'm sorry," Mack replied, "I don't think I heard you."

"What color is your hair under the wig?" he asked Betty.

"I am a brunette actually," she answered. "Why?"

Betty started to take her wig off, but Mack said, "Dear, please don't do that." She stopped and put it back on.

The rabbi leaned in toward them. "This is going to sound totally crazy, and I have wondered about it for years! About five years ago, I had this extremely vivid dream, of pretty much the basis for this very meeting. I thought Miriam looked familiar. I think I finally understand the dream now."

Mack and Betty looked at each other, then back at the rabbi.

He continued, "The woman in my dream said her Hebrew name was Miriam Elisheva, similar to one of my relatives so I remembered it. In the dream, she had brunette hair. It was as though she spoke to my very soul. This dream was so profound, I could not get it out of my head for weeks." He went to his door to make sure nobody was around.

"Now normally today, we do not take dreams to have much meaning, even though our sages say that dreams can be one-sixtieth of prophecy. But this was so real, it shook me up. The woman in my dream told me she was carrying twins, and that her husband's name was Maccabee. Then she said so emphatically, 'Please have compassion on my babies.' "

"Let me guess?" He looked at Mack with his eyebrows raised. "You are Maccabee? It is a highly unusual name."

"Well, yes. That was my legal name before our relocation," Mack whispered. "My late wife's Hebrew name was Miriam Elisheva. That's the name she took." Mack motioned at Betty.

Rabbi Silverstein realized he was scheduled for other things. He held up his finger, and called the secretary, asking her to reschedule everything to a different day. He found this all fascinating but needed to know how in the world to proceed. He was bound by Jewish law to uphold tradition, but he also wanted to help Mack, Betty, and their children in any way that he could. He needed to know more information.

"Miriam, please tell me a little bit about yourself."

Betty looked at Mack and he nodded it was okay to tell him.

"I was originally created to be a Caring Corporation caregiver model. Do you know much about Caring Corp.?"

He answered, "A little. They make prosthetics and robots?"

"We prefer to be called 'man-mades' or 'models,' but yes, that was how I was originally created. Then Dr. Robert Kerring who's like my brother, did an adjustment allowing me to change my core programming to learn more. But I went into this strange trance-like state. When I came out of it my programming had been tweaked, and I found I had emotions."

"Robbie, or Robert, looked into my coding one day and discovered it now had a series of letters, which he identified as being Michael's late wife Miri's DNA and part of the babies' DNA."

The rabbi sat there listening totally fascinated, with his elbows on his desk and his chin propped up with his fists.

"It was Hashgacha Pratit enough that I had Miri's face. Models' faces are based on decedents. Out of the millions of people who had died, I could have had anyone's face. But no, I had Miri's! Then I met Michael here when I was working as a flight attendant. He couldn't believe his eyes. Later, when I was kidnapped and nearly died being underwater, my life flashed before my eyes, but it wasn't only mine, some of it was Miri's. I told Michael something I saw in these visions, and it was something only he knew but I didn't. We sincerely believe that I have Miri's soul. There is no other explanation! But how do we explain it if I, as a man-made, am thought to not possess a soul?" Betty then started whimpering.

"Oh Betty, Miriam!" Mack slipped up. "Please don't cry, I know it is so frustrating."

"And you can see that she certainly has emotions! To top it off, my rabbi told me I shouldn't be in the room alone with her around Jews. You know, due to it looking bad–Marit Ayin. I love her with all my heart. But I have never laid a hand on her."

"I have not touched her even once. Do you know how hard it is to live with someone you love, and never even touch them? And she was not built like normal women, so we must be platonic. But it would be nice to at least touch each other!"

Mack could hold back his feelings no longer. "I'm so sorry Rabbi Silverstein. I have probably said far too much."

"Michael, I understand completely. Whew, you must be a pillar of self-control!" Rabbi Silverstein admitted.

"Well, in the accident that took Miri's life, it also left me with nerve damage and unable to . . . have any more children," Mack said somewhat embarrassed, and turned a bit red.

"Oh yes, that was my next question. How is Miriam carrying your children? And she is man-made?" Rabbi Silverstein scratched his head with his yarmulke.

"There's a fertility center at Caring Corp. I discovered that Michael and his late wife had frozen embryos there. I arranged to surprise him and become a surrogate to bear his children. I wanted to give him as priceless a gift as he gave me with my freedom." Betty smiled lovingly at Mack.

"So now, even though it is the short version, believe it or not, you know the basics of our whole story," Mack stated.

Rabbi Silverstein wished he could just marry them on the spot, but it was not in his power. There needed to be more rabbis involved, not to mention she needed to somehow at least have the status of a human convert. To decide such a thing, the

Jewish Court had to consist of three rabbis, and for a wedding, there must be a minyan, a group of ten men in attendance.

"I have a few ideas, but I need to consult some other rabbis. I know you told me all of this in confidence, so I must make sure they agree to keep it confidential as well, which they would. But do I have your permission to share this? Otherwise, there is nothing I can do on my own no matter how much I would like to." The rabbi looked at them with such compassion. Betty could read him, and she agreed, then Mack did as well.

"Please, give me your number so I can contact you as soon as we figure something out. There are going to be many people in town for a big wedding here on Sunday. I am going contact the members of our local Jewish Court and decide what we can do for you both once and for all. Maybe we can do this tomorrow or Thursday. You deserve to have a happy and normal married life. Well, as much as you're able to. I can certainly say that I am glad to not be in your situation."

Rabbi Silverstein escorted them out of the office to leave.

"Did you want to take a little tour of our shul?" he asked.

"Sure," both Betty and Mack answered together.

"Let's go to the social hall. My wife is helping set things up in there. She makes such beautiful table settings. Esther, come meet our newest members!" He motioned his wife over. She wore a wavy brown-haired wig and was very perky.

"Hi Mrs. Silverstein, my name is Miriam Elisheva Gold."

"Rebbetzin, a rabbi's wife is called a rebbetzin," Mack whispered very softly next to Betty's ear so only she could perceive it with her enhanced hearing.

Nice to meet you, Rebbetzin Silverstein!" Betty said. "Your synagogue is very nice."

"Good recovery, that was perfect," Mack whispered, he was looking down and smiling, hoping nobody else had noticed him.

"Thank you, Miriam. How are you today?" Esther asked.

Mack whispered, "Say, 'Baruch HaShem.'" He and the rabbi left to talk some more, since Mack thought Betty was doing well enough on her own. "I think you'll be okay now."

"Baruch HaShem," Betty repeated as instructed. She had heard Mack say it before, but looked up the definitions in her mind anyway to be sure of the meaning and context:

"Baruch HaShem." Hebrew; Translation: Literally, "Blessed is The Name," or figuratively, "Blessed is The Creator." Definition: Standard reply of a religious Jew meaning that one is doing well; alternately, a response to receiving good news.

She was "Bettying-out", and the rebbetzin noticed she was staring into space. "Are you sure about that?"

"Yes. I'm sorry. I have been a bit spacy lately," Betty replied as she rubbed her small baby bump.

"Oh, perfectly understandable," Rebbetzin Silverstein said. "You can just call me Esther. I don't really like being called 'Rebbetzin.' My husband and I are very informal here."

Esther continued, "We like people to feel comfortable and at home. It's fine to call him Rabbi, but we don't like all that addressing us in third person. Save the respect for HaShem!"

Betty was very worried about drawing attention to herself and not fitting in. Mack had been so concerned about her potentially being viewed as a machine that she was starting to feel anxious. She was fighting her own emotions of anxiety.

"Are you sure you're okay? There is a special guest room down the hall if you would like to go lie down for a bit," Esther said with a look of concern on her face.

"No, no, I'm fine. I think our trip and everything being so new is just a bit overwhelming. The babies shifted their position a little while ago," Betty was not really thinking things through as well as she usually did.

"You can feel that? How do you know? You must be super-perceptive and very in touch with your body."

"Indeed, I am," Betty said proudly. "I mean, I can tell what goes on inside of myself more than average. Could you please tell me where the ladies' room is Esther?"

Esther pointed beyond the doors of the social hall.

Betty thanked her and went into the restroom. She was starting to have nearly the equivalent of a panic attack. Her processors were accelerating to almost maximum capacity, making her simulated heartbeat and breathing sounds speed up unusually fast. She felt so uneasy without Mack.

Chapter 23

Hiding Out in the Restroom

Once in the restroom, Betty texted Mack in her mind with his new number, and they conversed for a while:

"Michael, I don't think things are going so well, can you please come back?"

```
"Miriam Dear, maybe excuse yourself and
go home. Do more research on Hebrew words.
Aren't you preprogrammed for this?"
```

"I am programmed only for modern Hebrew that they speak in Israel. Some of these terms and phrases are so different, especially with the subtle pronunciation differences between European 'Ashkenazi', and Israeli 'Sefardi' Hebrew. It's like the difference between British English and a southern drawl. Both are English, but sound very different. I'll have to create a database from scratch, since some people even use Yiddish mixed in."

Betty started whimpering and losing confidence.

"I don't know if I can do this. I am afraid I'll blow our covers! Should we tell the rebbetzin our story too?"

```
"I don't think that's necessary. Woody
said as few people as possible should
know. Where are you?"
```

"I'm hiding out in the women's restroom."

"You can't stay in there for too long,
she may try to come in and check on you
to see if you're alright."

"She already suspects that I'm not feeling very well."
"Just do the best you can. Be friendly.
You usually are to everyone anyway. If
it's too hard, go back home."

"I'll go try again some more. Thank you, Michael."

Betty came out of the bathroom and went over to Esther.

"Are you feeling any better now?" Betty read Esther's expressions and body language very carefully. She saw she was totally sincere, and truly concerned for her welfare.

"Yes. I guess I am just not used to being pregnant," she whispered. "Do you need any help setting up?" Betty asked, "The table settings are stunning! What is the occasion?"

Esther replied, "There's a wedding on Sunday; a young couple. The Kallah is a newer member here. We are so pleased, Hannah is a delightful girl, very quiet. And Reuven the Chattan, is from the UK. They're going to live here in Midwood!"

Esther obviously thought Betty to be just another average Jewish woman, since she spoke to her like a "native."

Oh goodness, Betty thought to herself. *I'm going to have to speed up my processors so as not to "Betty-out" and research extra quickly. Kallah = bride; and Chattan = groom.*

"I have things under control here, but they may need help

in the kitchen," Esther said. "Here, I'll introduce you to the ladies. It is almost always the same volunteers every time."

Betty tagged along to the large commercial kitchen, with stainless steel counters and separate double ovens, one each for meat and dairy, as was the custom for kosher food.

Esther introduced Betty. "Ladies, this is Miriam Elisheva, she just moved into the neighborhood. Miriam, this is Rina, Tovah, Tamar, and Sharona. She pointed to each one as she said their names. They are my regular helpers. We all enjoy the fruits of their labors. Rina is basically in charge of the kitchen here anyway, and she makes most of the food. Would you like to sample some of the fresh cookies they just baked?"

"Oh, I'm sorry. I am on a highly specialized diet," Betty replied, slightly changing her usual response. "But they do look so delicious. I would love to try them if I could."

"No worries. My mother has a nut allergy, so I understand completely. She'll be coming to stay with us when this one is born. I'm expecting my sixth," she whispered, as she rubbed her own small baby bump. "I'm getting bad hunger pangs. I'm just so hungry, but I'd hate to eat in front of you."

"That's perfectly alright Esther. I'm used to people eating in front of me. I think nothing of it because I don't really get hungry. My husband has to eat in front of me as well, and it took him some time to get used to once we were married."

"Thank you, Miriam. That makes me feel much better."

Esther picked up one of the cookies, said a blessing on it and took a bite. "Mmm! Delicious." She put her hand to her mouth and daintily tried to keep any crumbs from scattering.

"So, how long have you two been married? And these are your first? You said 'babies' so are you having twins or triplets?" Esther was comfortable with Betty already.

Betty smiled responding, "Twins, a boy and a girl. I don't have room for more than two!" They both laughed, but Betty realized that most women didn't usually have a choice.

Thankfully, Betty had gotten out of the question as to how long they had actually been married.

"I like you, Miriam. You have a great sense of humor. I think you'll fit in here just fine." Esther chuckled.

"Baruch HaShem," Betty said her newly learned phrase. She hadn't really meant it to be funny, and hoped she wouldn't say anything else to make them suspicious. Betty decided to try to act like them, and offered to help them chop onions. However, she didn't realize how they affected most humans.

"Whew, these red onions are so strong! How do you do it Miriam, I just can't stop crying, ha-ha-ha", Rina said, wiping her eyes with a nearby napkin, and sniffling quite a lot.

"I guess I'm not very sensitive to them," Betty replied. "Would you like me to chop your onions for you?"

"Sure, here's a knife. Be careful, it's new and very sharp."

Rina started to hand her the knife, but it slipped right out of her wet hand. Betty, with her super-fast reflexes caught the knife by the blade and sliced the inner parts of her fingers, through her skin layers almost to her tactile sensor layer.

Feeling just terrible, Rina apologized profusely. Betty, knowing how she healed rapidly, convince Rina that it was only a little nick. In comparison to her stab wound it was. She quickly wrapped her hand with a napkin and excused herself to go home before anyone could notice she wasn't bleeding.

She thanked them for a good time, waved goodbye, and left.

Betty texted Mack in her mind: *"I cut myself and went home."*

Mack now rushed home asking, "Are you okay Dear? How's your cut?" He tried to talk to her and comfort her. Betty was visibly down, and not herself. He was very concerned.

"My cuts will heal in a day, don't worry," she answered.

"What happened, what went so wrong?" he asked.

"I don't think I fit in Michael. I'm used to working in a kitchen alone, and I don't cry when onions are chopped, and I don't bleed when I'm cut, and I guess I'm just . . . not feeling very human right now! I quickly covered my wounds, but how do I explain these things? If I really am Miri, shouldn't I be fitting in here better?" She whimpered. "I feel so awkward! It seems like every single event, all holidays and celebrations, it all centers around food. And I can't eat, or it will kill me!"

"Honey, it's okay. Nobody can remember their past lives. You can't expect to just suddenly pick up where Miri left off!"

He wished he could just go hug her, but still wanted to stick to his stringencies. "I shouldn't have assumed that just because you're programmed to be able to speak Hebrew that you'd automatically be fine. I know, it's a whole different culture than what you're used to. You'll get there. Just try to find things in common with the other ladies."

Mack tried to reassure her. "I had a nice talk with the rabbi, and he's going to see if he can do something with two other rabbis. I think things will work out to our benefit. Maybe you should go and charge and sleep for a bit."

Out of desperation, Mack tried to contact the rabbi again.

"I'm so sorry to bother you Rabbi Silverstein, this is Michael Gold again, I know you're probably very busy with the wedding coming up, but do you have a minute to talk?"

"Sure, Michael. I know it can be difficult to settle into a new place," the rabbi tried to console him.

"It's Miriam. She is feeling very awkward. Every place she's gone she has fit in, until now. I feel so bad for her. All her closest friends knew that she was man-made, but here, she is terrified everyone would think of her as just a machine without a soul, and she can't tell anyone about it anyway to protect her identity. I think I worried about it so much, that it weighed heavily on her heart. Well, you know what I mean."

"I understand Michael. It must be very hard for her. I can tell you the ideas I have if it will make you feel better."

Chapter 24

This Too Is for the Best

"Please Rabbi Silverstein, tell us any ideas you may have. My little family is suffering!" Mack implored him.

The Rav answered, "With all you have told me about the unexplainable DNA in the computer coding, and what I experienced with my dream, I truly believe that Miriam has the soul of your late wife. I know it sounds totally crazy in our world of traditions since she is man-made. But I'm hoping that we can do some rather 'unorthodox' procedures." He chuckled.

"They would still be within Jewish law but should give her the status of being considered as much like a real human woman as possible. Would you like me to talk to her?"

"Oh, could you please? I think she feels comfortable with you since you know her true man-made origins."

"You and Miriam can come to my office later. We'll talk then. I need to go, but thanks for calling," he said cheerily.

Mack really liked Rabbi Fishel Silverstein. He was very understanding, even more so than his old rav. It seemed that everything happened for a reason, and up to this point, it had all worked out for the best.

Mack and Betty went to meet Rabbi Silverstein after the evening prayers at his office. He shut the door and sat down to talk with them.

"I had an idea. Now, I believe that you Miriam, have Michael's late wife's soul. My train of thought is this . . ."

He stroked his beard as he thought. It reminded Betty a bit of Dr. Kerring.

"You know how cookware and converts to Judaism are made 'spiritually Jewish' by dunking them into the water of the special ritual bath called a mikveh?"

Mack nodded yes and Betty cocked her head inquisitively.

"There are two different aspects we are talking about. The physical and the spiritual. I hope you can follow me."

Mack and Betty leaned forward listening closely.

"Miriam, your man-made body is essentially a vessel to carry the children. It becomes physically Jewish by dunking it in the mikveh. A person's soul also becomes Jewish as they dunk in the mikveh. I figure, if you get in that mikveh, you'd be covered either way," he announced excitedly.

"Once that occurs, you two can go through a Jewish marriage ceremony. Only a being with a soul can have a legitimate marriage. But then, your status of being a person in the spiritual realm can't be questioned!" He wagged his finger.

"Can you please explain what takes place?" Betty asked.

"Certainly Miriam. There are three elements to a Jewish marriage." He counted them out on his fingers. "A contract, a gift of some value, and the couple must be secluded together in a lockable room for at least eight minutes."

Rabbi Silverstein continued, "There was once a case where there was a children's play that was put on for an audience of parents. In this play, the boy proposed, the girl accepted, and there was a whole wedding ceremony." He smiled slightly, but still had a serious expression on his face.

"It turned out that because the play had all three elements of an actual marriage, the two children literally had to get a real divorce. That is how strict and serious this Jewish law is!"

Rabbi Silverstein got up and was pacing, gesturing as he thought out loud. He was growing confident that it could work.

"First, we can sign a plain paper Ketuba with witnesses, having the current date. People can assume the old decorative one you display in your home is the current one, and that you have already been married for some time." Mack and Betty listened to him and nodded.

"Second, we hold a ceremony in which Michael, you give the gift of a ring to Miriam saying a special statement that she is consecrated to you only. Then third, you both enter a room alone, as witnesses watch you close the door." He clapped his hands together, turning toward them saying, "All three elements have taken place, so it would be legally binding!"

They grinned, realizing how hard Rabbi Silverstein was working to make their situation comply with everything possible. He continued pacing and talking.

"As long as you're married to each other under Jewish

law, Miriam, you would not be considered an unwed mother, which of course is forbidden. But the children were created at the Caring Corp. center at the time when Michael and his late wife were already married! We're doing this all for the children's sake, and the mock-wedding will be kept completely confidential to protect your identities." All three smiled at each other realizing it could really work.

"However, the big problem is, I need two other rabbis for the spiritual part. All conversions to Judaism must be observed by three rabbis." The rabbi paused for a short time.

Betty noticed he exhibited some micro-expressions that showed he was somewhat concerned about it.

"Now if you Miriam, and you Michael really love each other, which I can tell just by looking at you both that you do, I think this is a way that under Jewish law, it could be considered a real, legitimate marriage. And then, you can finally touch each other without question."

Betty beamed after that statement. She and Mack looked at each other with loving eyes and smiled from ear to ear.

"You don't know how much of a hugger Miriam here is. We've both had to exert a lot of self-control." Mack smiled.

Rabbi Silverstein grinned, raised his eyebrows and asked, "What do you think of my ideas so far?"

"They sound incredible, Rav! We can't thank you enough!" Mack stood up and shook his hand.

"Just hang in there guys and cheer up Miriam. I think once you have your babies, you will fit in a lot better too."

"Over the next two days, I'll need to contact the two other rabbis and have a final meeting with them to see if we can make this all work. That will be the key. But you know the old saying, 'two Jews, three opinions.' Trying to get everybody on the same page can be a real challenge."

The next day, one of the members of the Jewish Court, Rabbi Levi Hadad had an appointment to come to Rabbi Silverstein's office. Mack and Betty, almost literally bumped into Rabbi Hadad, who was coming along quickly because he was running late. He saw Betty's face and stopped cold, exclaiming, "Et ha-isha she-eriti be-chelomi lifnei chamesh shanim!"

He was a Sefardi Rabbi who spoke Israeli-style Hebrew that Betty could understand. She processed it in her mind: *"You are the woman I saw in my dream five years ago!"*

They sat down and talked together in the office, and the whole exchange was strikingly similar to what Rabbi Silverstein had related to them before. Rabbi Hadad also had part of a message revealed to him in his dream, which he too remembered vividly. Now, two out of three rabbis were completely in favor of doing the whole unusual procedure.

The third and final rabbi was the oldest, and the head of the Jewish Court. Rabbi Zalman Ungar was a very strict,

Ultra-Orthodox rav, and he would be the one to need the most convincing, since he rejected most modern technology.

Rabbi Silverstein called Rabbi Ungar on the phone. He knew he didn't have a computer, or even a smart phone that could display video images for communication.

"Rav Ungar! How are you?" . . . "Good. Would you have some time for a brief conference? I need to set up a meeting for the three of us tomorrow morning. It's a very urgent matter that must be dealt with immediately." Rabbi Silverstein tried speaking to his heart first.

"There are children involved." . . . "It's not a divorce, but more like a conversion situation. You could almost say that it is much like the pregnant wife has had a brain transplant." . . . "Well, no. That level of technology is not exactly available yet today, but please just hear me out. The woman was not born in the normal manner of women."

He tried very hard not to elaborate too much. . . . "No, not a C-section or in-vitro." . . . "There is one other way, I'll explain it in the meeting." Rabbi Silverstein started sweating, and was getting very nervous.

"Oh, you need to go now? Can we please schedule an official meeting for tomorrow morning?" . . . "Excellent. Let's meet at my office here at shul. Rabbi Hadad has already agreed to be here. How is 9 a.m.?" . . . "Great."

"By the way, there's a couple getting married here Sunday,

if your wife would like to provide some of her delicious pastries." . . . "Oh, she already made them? Wonderful! Well, I'll see you tomorrow then. Thank you, Rav Zalman."

The rabbis ended their call. Rabbi Silverstein happily sighed, then confirmed the meeting with Rabbi Levi Hadad.

"Okay Rav Levi, we're on for tomorrow at 9 a.m. I didn't go into too much detail, but I'm hoping if Rav Zalman sees the couple there in person it will be more impactful. It's always much better to physically see the people, then you realize how you are directly affecting their lives. We'll do the best we can with HaShem's help. Thank you so much."

Now that the meeting was arranged for the next day, it had to be a unanimous vote or there simply was nothing Rabbi Silverstein could do. He called up Mack next.

"Michael, good news! The meeting is all set up for tomorrow morning after services, at 9 a.m. Please have Miriam come. I am hoping that if Rabbi Ungar sees her, he will realize the gravity of his decision. He is the last one to vote, and he is going to be a tough cookie to convince. Rabbi Hadad and I will do the best that we can, but it is in HaShem's hands. We must daven about it. We'll see you both tomorrow."

Betty heard their conversation, and analyzed the word in her mind, *"Daven." Yiddish; Translation: "To pray."*

Betty and Mack looked into each other's eyes lovingly.

"I think we are in good hands," Betty said to Mack. "We are going to have such a bright and happy future. A new life, full of the wonders of childhood and the potential challenges of raising twins." She couldn't wait! Her longing to have a real family of her very own could truly become a reality.

However now, their precious future would be up to the decision of this unknown Rabbi Zalman Ungar. If the verdict of the Jewish Court would deem Betty to have a soul, then she, Mack and their children could finally have a normal existence, just like any other family.

On the contrary, if for some reason he would think she did not possess a soul, what would become of their lives? Would they be exposed and exiled within the Jewish community? Would she be deemed a machine, unworthy to keep her identity a secret and enabling Gio to find out she was alive after all? They both shuddered to think of such consequences.

Their future would remain to be seen. Until then, Betty and Mack hoped and prayed that Rabbi Silverstein could convince the head rabbi of her true status of having Mack's late wife Miri's soul. Only then could they and their family be free to live out their lives in love, peace, and happiness. And that was still their plan.

Visit **ManMadeBook.com**

Enjoy the
MAN-MADE
TRILOGY

Meet all your favorite characters
from each of the books, as they
all come to life in pictures!
Visit some of their special
hangouts.

Take a virtual tour of Caring
Corp. where it all started.

See scenes from each of
the Man-Made books.

(To eliminate spoilers, view them
in order and don't peek ahead.)

Other Books by Cassie Cluster

Potty Training for REAL Cats:
Toilet Training for Humans & Felines
Picky Press 2021

Man-Made - One of a Kind
Picky Press 2024

Man-Made - Three out of Four
Picky Press 2024

CassieCluster.com

PickyPress.com